Gunsmoke empire

DATE DUE

6/2013			

This Large Print Book carries the
Seal of Approval of N.A.V.H.

GUNSMOKE EMPIRE

JACKSON COLE

WHEELER PUBLISHING

A part of Gale, Cengage Learning

GALE
CENGAGE Learning

Detroit • New York • San Francisco • New Haven, Conn • Waterville, Maine • London

GALE
CENGAGE Learning

LIBRARY OF CONGRESS CATALOGING-IN-PUBLICATION DATA

Cole, Jackson.
 Gunsmoke empire / by Jackson Cole.
  pages ; cm. — (Wheeler Publishing large print western)
  ISBN 978-1-4104-5574-1 (softcover) — ISBN 1-4104-5574-2 (softcover)
 1. Large type books. I. Title.
 PS3505.O2685G8667 2013
 813'.52—dc23   2012043024

Published in 2013 by arrangement with Golden West Literary Agency.

Printed in the United States of America
1 2 3 4 5   17 16 15 14 13

Gunsmoke Empire

Chapter I
Hills of Death

The gentle west wind rose over the wooded summits of the great southwest mountains, impartially caressing both the good and the evil. It sighed through the glossy-leaved stands of live-oak and virgin pine forming the watershed of the Maravilla River, whose system extended hundreds of miles eastward, sustaining a large and prosperous people. It cooled the sweated hides of grazing livestock, growing fat for the market.

To the wind rose a rasping shriek, the groans of small, dark-skinned slaves, toiling with ax and saw, blindly destroying through the feverish, greedy desire of man, the lives of a multitude. Brute overseers, armed with guns and whips, lashed the helpless peons on.

A wide, squat man, whose bulging muscles showed his terrific strength, hurried through the bleeding forest. "Bigjaw" Dave Haley, boss muleskinner, wore no hat on his shaggy carrot-topped head; red-rimmed eyes burned in his misshapen face, jaw prominent and covered by a thick, rusty stubble. He carried a blacksnake whip with leaden tippets that cut deep gashes in quivering flesh. Corduroy pants, flannel shirt open, showing a hairy barrel chest matted by sweat, and big hobnail shoes completed his get-up. A cut of tobacco bulged out one cheek.

With his grizzly gait he ambled up to a slender, foppishly clad man standing on a fallen giant oak's raw stump. "Hey, Ross! That dude's bin talkin' to the Mexes and I jest seen him writin' in a book!"

Valentine Ross's greenish eyes slitted; he gulped as though his soul distilled a vitriol of hate that seared his throat. He had a face like death, bony sharp, pasty-white despite his outdoor life. Between cruel, ribbon-thin lips he clipped a saliva-stained cigarette. Taller than Haley he weighed half as much, with sharp shoulders and protruding bones. His gray trousers, slim black shoes on dainty feet of which he was inordinately proud, were very neat as was his white shirt with string tie, and lain dark felt hat that was carefully placed on oiled black hair.

"And the Boss is coming tonight," he snarled.

So ferocious was Ross that, though any of the huge, fierce lumberjacks could have broken him in two with their hands, he dominated them and they feared him as they might the devil. For weapons he carried two small-calibre pistols and a narrow keen-edged knife.

Bigjaw's voice was a bear's bass growl; Ross's a penetrating, ill-tempered rasp with a hint of accent. He had mestizo blood, with the worst qualities of both races.

Through the cut forest might be seen slaving Mexicans, faces drawn with anguish, emaciated ribs visible through tatters of clothing. When Valentine Ross moved off his stump, dark eyes rolled fearfully; as Ross passed a group at a rotating saw, he struck out at a peon who was rocking dizzily, plainly sick. The man jumped back with a shriek of terror, the saw snapped up his shirt and in a second it was over, the peon bleeding to death in the mound of sawdust.

Ross did not look back. He moved with a serpent's supple glide, Haley rolling at his heels. They crossed a mountain stream and came to the camp, mostly huts built of logs. A young man in a blue suit, his curly head bare, quickly came out of a shack marked "OFFICE: SOUTHWEST LUMBER CO." But he was not quick enough, for Ross had seen him. He tried to look unconcerned but Ross gulped as he stared into his victim's eyes. He ordered coldly:

"Give me the book."

The young fellow was rattled. "Why, what —" he began.

Ross's signal was imperceptible to the victim; Haley's whip swished, tippets cracking like a gunshot, tearing the young man's eyes. He screamed in agony and Haley rushed at him, threw him, driving a knee into his belly. Bigjaw took a small notebook from the writhing man's pocket and handed it to Ross.

Ross scanned the pages. Then he leaped, snatching up Haley's whip, and began to slash the helpless victim, beat him with a mad strength that made Bigjaw stare in awe.

"This is what spies get!" Ross shrieked. Tiring when he had cut the victim almost to death he threw down the lash, drew a pistol and fired three shots into the dying man.

A horseman, a lean fellow with a cheek badly scarred from an old knife wound, came galloping in. "Hey, boss! Couple Bar W waddies headin' here!"

A short while later two cowboys rode up to an apparently deserted camp. One dismounted, picked a fresh hide from a pile near the racks where fresh beef hung draining.

"Bar W!" he said sharply. Ross emerged from the office. "Looka, yuh danged rustlin' dude," cried the Bar W hombre, "what yuh mean, butcherin' our cows! Yuh've stole too many from us Valley people and yuh got to pay."

"All right — here's your pay," Ross said, with a shrug that was a signal, for guns blasted from the bush into the waddies. The mustangs reared, dashed off through the trees.

Death rode there, wholesale death and horror; and death not only to men but to mighty Texas, threatened by the murderous lust of a man for power.

The west wind descended the eastern slope where the Maravilla swelled from a mountain stream to a wide river watering grassy plains. Through the river's calm beneficence men lived. The wind crossed the main river's valley to Bowietown, lying along the north bank, a typical cowtown with lines of wooden buildings, a big general store, "YAGER'S," and with rutted roads dried by the Texas sun. The wind rustled the trees of the Plaza in the middle of town to cool the excited faces of the crowd assembled there. On the wooden platform sat several of Maravilla's most important citizens, and the honest, toil-hardened Texans listened to their leaders.

Smiling Hank Yager, mayor of Bowie, presided at this indignation meeting. A bluff, square man, teeth easily showing in good humor, thick brown hair awry, brown shirt and pants tucked homily into half-boots, for like many outdoor men Yager liked to be on easy terms with people. His brown eyes were sun-seamed, and he spoke with the bluff heartiness of man to man.

"You heard what happened! Two Bar W men gunned up there this mornin'. Sam Ward's word is gold."

A giant of a man, in rancher's clothes, expensive boots and pants, great Stetson, leaped up, round, honest face red with anger. Sam Ward towered on the dais. He was a great cattle king of Maravilla, loved and respected, head of the Ranchers' Union. The Bar W backed on the western watershed, though the entire range was open and cows from the other outfits grazed the lush hills.

Ward had straight-looking blue eyes, wide-set over a nose once mashed by a horse's lashing hoofs; shoulders broad as a door, arms big as most men's legs. He was an outspoken fellow, a self-made man who had always taken care of himself and his own.

Behind Ward sat his pretty daughter Elsie. Her hair was darker than her father's but she had his wide blue eyes, fresh with youth; a dainty girl in white starched riding clothes. Her features were even, her whole look showed her earnest sweetness. Her face glowed with admiration as she watched her father.

"Boys," boomed Ward, "yuh know me. I come to this country when it was wilderness, nobody here but a few outlaws on the dodge. Done saved my cowboy wages up nawth and bought a quarter section and started with a few runts. Bin here thutty years last October and I have seen Maravilla develop into a wonder spot. We bin lucky here with fresh, plentiful water." He spoke with a simplicity that gripped the hearts of his listeners; they felt his intense love for home.

"I love this land. I jest couldn't live anywheres else. What's goin' on tears me bad as a knife. Them skunks up above are cuttin' off all them trees for miles in sech a hurry they've ruint the hills. They've stolen our cows and used our hosses to dig ditches and drag logs; they've gunned anybody who went up there." He banged a huge fist into his other hand. "We got to act! I'm for it pronto!"

A cheer went up. Alf Betts, town marshal, thumped his wooden leg on the boards. Mayor Yager gave the floor to a tall, gaunt gentleman.

"Senator Ardmore wants to talk, boys."

Senator Rathburn Ardmore stood six-feet-two; thin and angular, bony shoulders stooped in black frock coat. A heavy shock of iron-gray hair waved on his long, triangular head. He spoke with a trained orator's power.

"Gentlemen, perhaps the lumbermen are breaking the law, but is this any reason why we should? I counsel patience and legal means. Austin will help us. A complaint has already been sent the governor. Some of the stock stealing may be laid at the feet of the Mexican bandit, Vasco Torquila. Of course, I'm on your side; the Maravilla is my homeland, and I join with my dear friend Sam Ward, eager to serve you. That's why I caution you to stick by the law."

Mayor Yager stepped up. "Boys, I'm like Ward, in favor of vigilante action and quick. Let's go up and drive 'em out!"

The crowd began to shout and men hurried for their horses, checked their guns. Sam Ward and Mayor Yager rode in the van

14

as a hundred riders headed swiftly for the hills.

Near sundown in the heavily bushed foothills the winding trail came to a great ditch cut into red clay. Earth had been thrown out and the blood-red sun was in the posse's eyes as they bunched up to stare at this deep gully.

The quiet was shattered by a terrific gunfire. Fierce-faced men jumped up from behind the breastworks, and from the bushes at the sides, pouring a withering death into the massed riders. Horses reared as the startled ranchers went for their guns, scattering for cover. Half a dozen fell in the first awful volley. Valentine Ross's high whine, Bigjaw Haley's roar, could be heard shouting orders over the din. The battle opened, and Sam Ward was up front, down in a spewed mass of granite rocks, six-gun spitting hate for the men who were ruining his beloved country.

But the ambush had smashed them; and after a few moments, the fighting cowmen saw Mayor Yager stagger from the rock nest, with Sam Ward limp across his back, head hanging and dripping blood. Yager caught at a horse, dumped the cattle king's body across the saddle, leaped up behind. With a last defiant shot, the mayor rode his friend out of the battle.

Ward's finish disheartened the ranchers; they retreated, the rattled survivors taking to their mounts, harried for a mile by the victorious lumbermen.

Later, back at the Bar W, Elsie Ward stared in wide-eyed anguish at the death-pale face of her father. Yager and others had brought him home, laid him gently in his bed.

"Ride for the doctor, quick," Elsie gasped.

"Afraid he's gone," Yager growled, shaking his head. "Elsie, I'm sorry; I want to do everything I can to help you."

Bancroft Morton, leather creaking, whistled as he headed up into the hills on his pet horse, Black Rascal. He was a bronc buster, expert at taming wild mustangs, meandering from spot to spot in his work. Cool and quiet, Morton had amber eyes and a level gaze. He made a lean, handsome figure in his easy saddle. He wore expensive leather, for his equipment had to be good in such work. He had light, curly hair which he kept close-clipped.

Young, hardly more than a boy, but he was able to take care of himself in a hard world.

He was in the Ord Mountains, and he had been told in Oklahoma that they were full

16

of wild ponies or strays from the big valley outfits which would pay to have them captured and broken. But as he came in from the north, strange sounds, the shriek of saws, the dim yells of men, the ditch that ran for two miles below, made him swear in disgust.

"Mustangs'll never stick around here," he muttered. Over on the next ridge he saw the figures of toiling men; from a distance they looked exactly like ants.

The soft west wind was in his bronzed face as he sighted a band of horses. "Shore seem tame," he told Black Rascal. His pursuit of the horses took him near the other ridge, and too easily he trapped the horses in a natural corral.

He was disgusted, altogether. "Them lumberjacks are spoilin' this country," he growled.

He dismounted, took his rope, when a sharp command brought him facing about. On a bank nearby stood men, led by a thin, pasty-faced devil whose eyes gleamed green as a cat's. Morton didn't like their looks as they silently stared at him, "Howdy, gents," he sang out, "what's up — ?" The thin man whipped out a small pistol and then fired; the bronc buster felt the slug burn his ribs. It spun him about but he grabbed his Colt and let go at them. The horses stampeded and their bodies protected Morton as he quickly mounted and rode away hell-for-leather.

The next morning, his wound roughly bandaged, he sighted across rolling prairie where steers grazed thick, the low-lying buildings of the big Bar W. He pulled into the yard, before him the wide-sprawled ranch, a rambling, one-storied house, barns, bunkhouse, corrals, with the Maravilla River close at hand.

Ban Morton stopped at a rear corral; a tall hombre with a leathery, saturnine face looked slowly up at him.

"Howdy," Ban said. "My name's Morton. Say, who's boss here?"

"I am, Nevada Lewis," the saturnine hombre growled. What of it?"

Morton dismounted, stretched his legs.

He moved with the queer, stiff gait of the bronc buster, as though he were unused to walking.

A young woman appeared from a kitchen door and Ban Morton stared. In that first look at Elsie Ward, the world suddenly changed for Morton; his lips opened and he tensed. She went to a line, took down some fresh, clean bandage cloths, went back inside. There was such a dejected droop to her girlish figure Morton was deeply affected.

"Nevada" Lewis didn't miss his reaction. "Old Man's bad hurt," he said to Ban.

"Nevada," Ban Morton drawled, "I'd like to talk to whoever's runnin' the shebang here. It's important."

Lewis shrugged. "There's some gents inside if yuh want," he said coldly.

Morton stalked to the front porch and went up. The door was open and he came face to face with Elsie, as she was crossing toward a large side room. Through the doorway, Morton glimpsed a great figure flat in a bed, and several men sitting round him.

As Elsie stared into his eyes, Morton heard a deep voice growl, "While we were up after them skunks, Torquila raided the Dot O and Runnin' T thirty mile south. We got to do somethin' 'bout that Mex bandit. Nuthin's safe any more."

Ban took off his hat. "My name's Ban Morton, ma'am. I rode here special to warn yuh of what's goin' on up above, in the hills. Lumbermen up there are cuttin' yore timber off and it's goin' to ruin yore entire range."

"Thank you," said the young woman. She seemed to like Ban Morton's appearance and his honest voice. "Come inside — some of our friends are talking about what to do."

She led him to the side room and said:

"This is Ban Morton. Mayor Yager, Marshal Betts, my father, Sam Ward, Senator Ardmore —" She introduced the various ranchers of Maravilla, who watched the young stranger with a cold suspicion, until he started to speak to them.

"Gents," he began, "I saw what them lumbermen're up to. It's worse'n yuh know. Once they cut off all that timber it means yore whole range for hundreds of miles is ruined. Rains'll pour off the hills, gully yore land, carry off topsoil, yuh'll have floods when it rains, droughts when it don't, no river to speak of. I've seen it happen up nawth and it's terrible."

"What would you advise?" Yager boomed.

"Send a complaint direct to the guv'nor; the State won't allow sech destruction. Yuh'll need to act fast, too, or it'll be too late. S'pose, Miss Ward, yuh write it out and I'll take it to the telegraph office myself."

The ranchers were in dire straits, a whole people seeing the end of hope and life, with death bearing down on them.

20

Chapter II
A Ranger Hits the Trail

Cap'n Bill McDowell of the Texas Rangers, rugged old frontiersman that he was, whose hide was said to be tough enough to snap back at a Bowie knife, restlessly paced the confine of Austin Headquarters. He was in a disturbed mood.

"A terrible mess," he muttered, "and a big one."

He slammed a gnarled fist into a calloused palm. "Yessir, Hatfield's the on'y one kin handle it, if it can be done —"

A familiar tread caused him to swing, and he swore as his game leg twinged; too old to ride the Danger Trail now, Captain McDowell had a hard time holding himself in at news of atrocities against Texas.

"Hatfield!" he boomed, facing the cool, tall man who silently appeared before him.

Though six feet, Cap'n Bill had to look up to meet the gray-green, steady gaze of his star Ranger. Jim Hatfield was bronzed by wind and sun and rain, his rugged features quiescent but giving a hint of his terrific power. He had very wide shoulders, a lean-muscled body tapering to a fighting man's slim hips where hung two Colt .45s, blue-steel, that could flash into action with lightning speed.

"Yes, suh," he drawled.

At sight of Ranger Hatfield, at sound of that soft but compelling voice, McDowell felt reassured. He knew that the strength of a fighting panther was in that long body, that the heart beat with a flaming courage that never quailed.

Under the wide fawn Stetson showed jet-black, gleaming hair, the Ranger's whole mighty being radiating perfect health, steady nerves ever fully controlled. No man could match Jim Hatfield's speed in action and McDowell knew he had a diplomat's brain to coordinate with his marvelous physical power.

"Steel and hick'ry and coiled chain-lightnin'," McDowell thought as he eased down in the big fellow's company.

Hatfield's face was in repose softened by a wide, good-humored mouth but McDowell knew the deadliness with which the Ranger struck the enemies of Texas. In terse sentences the captain outlined the trouble gripping Maravilla.

"It's a big country, Jim, large as some eastern states. Puzzles me, too, how it's got so bad 'thout us hearin' much. Some complaints come in on this Vasco Torquila, the giant Mex bandit raidin' down there and I meant to send a man down. But this here land ruination Miss Elsie Ward speaks of in her personal telegram to the governor is new. Talks like we knowed all about it. Seems a passel of lumbermen 're cuttin' the timber off the Maravilla watershed and that concerns Texas. It's a big job in itself; but if private parties is allowed to cut timber thataway, there's no sayin' how far it'll reach. May mean ruination and anarchy in the state, so get goin'."

The cool Ranger's voice had a mildness to it that had fooled more than one blustering and now defunct gunman:

"Callate them hills 're where that forester disappeared, Cap'n!"

McDowell jumped, slammed the desk so the inkwell leaped. "By golly, Jim, yuh're right. Figgered mebbe he'd got hisself lost or gone over a cliff. But Sheriff George Godey of Brewster County wired he can't locate him. Yuh can trust Godey down there, he'll give yuh aid."

Hatfield didn't reply and McDowell

laughed inside. It was not the Ranger's way to ask aid; information was another thing, but when Jim Hatfield was ready he found a way to strike, strike with the unerring, deadly aim of a bullet.

"Been sev'ral murders there, of cowboys," added McDowell. "Elsie Ward's pa, Sam, was most kilt, the citizens went up to attack the lumbermen, had a battle, and got beat off, 'cordin' to Godey. It's bad when people take the law into their hands; yuh'll hafta straighten that out. And don't forget Vasco Torquila. Hustle now, hell's roarin' in Maravilla!"

Hatfield saluted; he asked no questions but strode out, door closing quietly behind him.

"Well," thought McDowell, "I'm glad it ain't me he's sicked on!"

In the brilliant sunshine Goldy, Hatfield's pet sorrel, nuzzled his master's hand, feigning to nip his sleeve, ears back. Hatfield's voice soothed the magnificent gelding, and he mounted, sitting the saddle with a master rider's ease. He carried his blue-steel Colts in oiled, supple holsters that would not drag; a Winchester snugged in a boot. The gray-green eyes shone for he was happiest when he was on his way, at work.

Jim Hatfield headed southwest for Maravilla and the legions of death.

While Jim Hatfield rode, a conference took place outside the office of the Southwest Lumber Company. The yellow moon peeped through the pines, and a ray struck the evil face of one who dominated the brutal crew.

"That bronc buster got word through," he growled, "and the Rangers know. They'll come."

"Let 'em," snarled a narrow-shouldered dude, tapping his knife. A bear-like hombre snapped a bullwhip.

"Watch," the chief insisted. "We need time, time to make our hook-up, get this timber out. Then we'll have control and to hell with everything. The Rangers 're the only thing we have to worry about. Fat Phil is taking care of Bowietown."

"Okay, anything you say, Chief, but you won't object if I call you up here to look at a dead body or two?"

"So long as it's not yours," and the chief grimly added, "the Rangers are a diff'rent proposition. I've done all I could to hold 'em off. Remember, I know more than you do, that's why you're workin' for me. I'll see to the Rangers myself."

"These ranchers are a nuisance," the dude growled. "I got fifty thousand foot of oak

and pine ready to go out; but they're am-
bushin' our teams to the railroad. We got to
be able to haul farther to the east now."

The chief cursed. "I'll break them, once
and for all," he declared furiously. "I must
have Maravilla, to hook up the whole shebang. I'll wipe that Union off the map!" . . .

Ranger Hatfield, on Goldy, both showing
the stains of their incredibly fast trip from
Austin, stared through the bush fringing the
bluff. Heading in for the Bar W and Bowietown, Hatfield had stopped at sight of the
chase across the plain. One man was fleeing
before a dozen, until the lanky fugitive's
lathered horse had hit a gopher hole and
crashed, sending the rider headlong in the
grass.

The angry voices of ranchers who had
seized the fugitive had drowned out the
faint sounds of Hatfield's stealthy approach;
in the purple shadows cast by high mesquite
with star-white blooms and thorny granjeno
the Ranger saw them swarming about the
quaking prisoner.

"String him up!" a harsh voice insisted,
and the cry was chorused, echoing in the
verdant rangeland.

The sky was a ruby-red dome, the sun a
great ball on the western hills; steers grazed
beyond and insects hummed in the death of

the day. The aromatic odor of sage and creosote tinged the exhilarating, sweet air.

"There's a good oak tree over there," a cowboy growled. "We'll teach yuh lumberjacks a lesson yuh won't forget!"

Hatfield was intrigued. He ran a long-fingered, slim hand down the line of his fighting jaw.

"So," he mused, "he's from up there! And I callate these'll be Bar W hombres takin' revenge." An idea had come to his clever brain, and he swung a booted foot to the earth, touching Goldy's muzzle to warn the sorrel to stand quiet.

Silently Jim Hatfield moved up to where he looked directly down on the necktie party. The victim, held by a dozen men in cowboy garb of Stetson, chaps and boots, wore a corduroy suit and he had lost his helmetlike corduroy hat when he fell; the Ranger noted his mutilated cheek. His sunken eyes rolled in terror and he shook at the imminence of lynch death.

"Don't, gents, please. I'm innocent."

"Innocent, hell!" a rancher snarled, slapping him. "I seen yuh myself up in the hills when Sam Ward was ambushed. We're goin' to string up every one of yuh we snaffle. Yuh was spyin' around the Bar W jest now. Why, that hoss yuh was on has a Bar W

27

brand on. That's 'nuff to hang yuh."

They weren't wasting any motions. A 40-foot lariat had been strung and tossed over the limb of a high oak tree close to the bluff where Hatfield crouched.

"He may not deserve savin'," thought Hatfield, "but I need a quick introduction and this looks like it." He had made his decision and action came instantly with it. He was not the man to miss such a chance to obtain information; the only hitch was the fact that he did not wish the ranchers to identify him as yet.

Hatfield did not descend among them but stayed back among the bushes, on the commanding eminence of the bluff, where rotted shale formed a slide. He drew his two six-guns, and the clicks as they cocked under his thumbs were lost in the shuffle. But the incisive command he uttered froze every man in the circle.

"Reach, gents!"

These were men who knew what a gun meant. Hands reached high even before their eyes rolled around. In the gathering gloom they saw the glow of the Lone Wolf's eyes, the glint of the hypnotizing Colts.

Hatfield kept his voice gruff; the intervening bush effectually hid him.

"Sorry to spoil yore party," he drawled.

"You, Scarface, grab that big chestnut and pull him up here." His all-seeing eye caught the slight move of a cowman who thought he was hidden behind a comrade's body. A six-gun barked and the bullet spat through Hatfield's Stetson crown. The echo was the Rangers gun, roaring blue-yellow, and the hombre uttered a sharp yelp:

"Shot my gun outa my hand!"

The precision shot jolted all idea of resistance out of them, and they just waited, as the lean hombre willingly shoved from the death ring, grabbed the rein of the powerful horse Hatfield had indicated, and came scrabbling up the slide.

"What now?" Scarface gasped, as though the rope already cut off his breath.

"Mount and ride. I'll follow."

The instant Hatfield swung, the cowmen went for their guns and fired into the bushes where he had crouched. The slugs snapped the leaves, but the angle prevented them from striking the Ranger as he mounted Goldy, swung and galloped after the man he had saved.

"Quickest way for a look-see up there," he mused, as Goldy loped in the swift trail west taken by Scarface.

The pursuit was begun. The Bar W men yanked their mustangs up the slide and came hell-for-leather on the trail, whooping it up and firing wildly. Hatfield had made a good choice; the chestnut could run like the wind and Goldy had to spread himself to stay at the flying hoofs. They ran several hundred yards before the infuriated lynching bee really started, and the pair in front began to gain for they could zigzag through the rising, bushy hills.

The last rays of day died and they rode for miles under a rising yellow moon. The ranchers finally quit in disgust, unable to trail wraiths in the night.

Panting, the scar-faced hombre swung in his saddle, eyes rolling in his narrow head.

"Thanks, mister. Yuh saved my life."

"Okay," drawled the Ranger. "I been too close to it myself to let a man stretch hemp."

Scarface seized this hint that the big man on the golden horse might be outside the law. He began to draw out Hatfield in what he thought a subtle manner, about his past. The Ranger by his terse replies let Scarface gain the impression he was on the dodge.

It was subtly done and Scarface, too, felt grateful, with the noose so close behind.

"Say, mebbe we kin use you. What's yore name?"

"They call me Frisco Jim."

"Okay, Jim. Tag along with us and you'll

30

be in clover. We're goin' to take Texas to hell 'fore we're through, and there's plenty in it." Scarface, wiping the sweat of death from his lean cheeks, was boastful.

"How use me?" asked the Ranger — he would draw out Scarface if possible but could not damage his standing by showing too much curiosity.

A look that was near to fear came over Scarface's countenance. He seemed to draw back and he muttered, "*He'll* tell you, Jim. Take my word for it, there's money and good money."

Plainly Scarface was a subordinate and afraid to talk too much. Hatfield shrugged, aware that he must step carefully or Scarface might grow suspicious.

A million stars powdered the sky. A million night creatures sang a song of mystery. The brush and trees rustled in the softness of the wind and beyond, the river placidly flowed through the gorgeous valley it created. Far up above, ahead, Hatfield saw tiny yellow specks in the forest that were lights.

It was midnight when they reached the camp of the Southwest Lumber Company. Alert guards patrolled the trail; three times were they challenged as they rode the fragrant, winding ways. From the dense thickets a hard voice demanded:

"Yes? Who's that?" The intonation was staccato, each word carefully articulated.

And each time Scarface replied the same way, by rote: "S. — W. — L.!" The two riders went through.

They forded the stream, up onto the space where stood the shacks. Hatfield looked over the camp. Fully awake men, with rifles, stood about, and through the trees he saw more dark figures, silver sheen of moonlight on gun barrels, by what seemed to be a large stockade. A few yards before the central hut, marked, "OFFICE. SOUTHWEST LUMBER CO." burned a red fire; lanterns hung on wooden pegs in the logs.

As the two dismounted, turned their horses into a rope corral, a bony figure slid from the office.

Danger was here, permeating the scented air of the pine woods. Hatfield could smell it. Hundreds of guns were ready to turn on him. The eerie shadows, grim faces under corduroy helmets, powerful figures in pants of the same material and gray flannel shirts, and a confused moaning that came from the stockade, would have shaken most men. Hatfield, cool, unperturbed, but alert, took in what he could.

The pasty-faced devil staring at Hatfield snapped, "Scarface! Who's that with you?"

Hatfield didn't like the voice any more than the man's appearance. It was an unpleasant, penetrating snarl, but plainly the dudish-clad hombre was a power in the camp.

"Ross," cried Scarface, "this big jigger saved me. I connected with our man at the ranch. It's fixed to cook Ban Morton, he's good as dead. But when I was leavin' a Bar W waddy reckernized me and they had the rope hung when this feller stuck guns on 'em. I won't go down that way no more, boss; they know me now. As for ridin' to Bowie and seein' Fat Phil, that's out too. Jim here's new; mebbe he can take over the job."

"Shut up," snarled Ross. "You'll do what you're told, Scarface." He stepped up to Hatfield, fixed his cattish eyes on the placid countenance of the officer, whose easy carriage was almost contemptuous, that of a reckless gunman who thinks he can take care of his hide. Indeed, Hatfield was figuring how much he could find out before Ross found him out. The ruby light glowed on the fish-belly skin of Ross's narrow face. Hatfield read him as a master foe, and he wondered how well Ross read him.

Beyond a brief glance at the shacks, at the dim outline of the stockade off among the

33

trees, Hatfield did not go; he was too clever to show curiosity.

For a moment the two men confronted one another and while not a move the Ranger made was wrong, Valentine Ross went as much by instinct as by appearance. But if the boss suspected anything he did not show it, beyond a gulp. He seemed to accept the tall jigger at Scarface's valuation.

Plenty of armed men around, watching the scene; at a word from Ross they would have run in to pour death into the Ranger. Scarface talked excitedly:

"Say, Ross, this feller kin move like light. He's on the dodge, name's Frisco Jim. Picked me away from them ranchers neat as you wish to see. I told him mebbe we could use him."

"Maybe we can," replied Ross smoothly. "You boys look worn out. Turn in, take your friend to that hut over there so you won't be disturbed." And to Hatfield he added, "Make yourself at home, pal. Welcome."

Was there, mused the Ranger, a sarcastic tinge to Ross's voice? He gravely thanked him. Crouched close at hand, in the shadows, he glimpsed a hogshead figure with rusty hair and beard; by his clothes, the blacksnake whip tucked under one arm, Hatfield guessed he was a muleskinner, and he heard Ross call him "Bigjaw."

Still Hatfield sensed the danger; he also sensed an expectancy. Save for the sough of wind in the trees, the peaceful murmur of Nature, faint crackle of the fire, there was quiet; then, as Hatfield swung to follow Scarface, a shrill, anguished shriek, the cry of a tormented soul, rang from the stockade in the woods; and a moment later two shots cracked, the voice ceased.

Hatfield looked there; then was aware Valentine Ross watched him. He shrugged, pretending to find nothing strange in this. The odor of fresh sawdust mingled with the smell of burnt wood; below, the Maravilla gurgled in its stony bed.

"C'mon," Scarface ordered nervously, touching his new pal's sleeve. "Let's turn in. I'm plumb wore out." He led the way along a path, north from the collection of huts to a log shack. Sleeping men were inside and Scarface found the Ranger a vacant bunk at the left of the doorway.

The Ranger lay down. Scarface closed the door. As the Ranger's eyes grew used to the gloom, the heavy breathing of sleepers in his ears, he noted the single small window a few feet away. He composed himself to wait, marshaling in his clever mind the events which he had observed. It was not his way to leap before making a thorough investigation and the set-up here looked huge, far-reaching.

It was not long before Scarface, wearied from fright, joined the snorers. The Ranger dozed, one ear open. About an hour later he heard sounds outside that brought him up on his elbow.

"Snap! Snap! Snap!" Not human sounds, those. "Whips," he decided. He heard cries of pain, and they were human. The stamp of many hoofs, the vibrations of the earth under the tread of many men and beasts, came through the bunk supports to his body.

"This is what Ross was expectin'," he thought, and silently rose, feet on the earth floor, and started for the window.

Scarface seemed asleep. Hatfield peered from the small, unglassed window opening and could see the fire near the office, and off to one side, Valentine Ross. The space before the office was crammed with men and animals, and Ross was talking to a man mounted on a great bay stallion, a giant form in flowing black serape, countenance shadowed by steeple-peaked sombrero gleaming with rows of pearl buttons.

All Hatfield could make of the Mexican's features were the darker blobs of mustache and beard; the spirited horse pivoted and the Ranger looked on the broad expanse of the rider's back as he spoke with Valentine Ross.

His eyes swept the armed, mounted gang of bandidos, an army of them on shaggy little Mexican mustangs; they slouched in the saddle as they pulled up at the South-west Lumber Company's camp. Small men, colorful in dress, with fancy boots adorned with great roweled spurs, those who wore boots, for some had spurs tied to their ankles, feet bare. Leather pants to protect the legs in the thorny chaparral; above the belt they looked like guerrilla soldiers, two X-crossed belts heavily laden with cartridges, side-arms of pistols and knife, rifle slung under a leg.

The majority favored the high pointed Mexican sombrero, though some wore old army felts. Fierce of face, with the cruelty of their Indian strains, raiders and killers by heritage, who followed the giant on the stallion.

They acted now as vaqueros though not herding cows but men, a massed column mounted on mules, hemmed in by the armed force. The victims cringed from the lashes wielded by the shrill-voiced bandidos. At a harsh command the peons swung toward the big stockade among the trees.

A cold fury hit Jim Hatfield. A glimmer of what the Southwest Company might be up to flashed across his brain. "Got to stop it," he muttered. And suddenly, engrossed in the strange proceedings outside, Hatfield realized he was not alone. Warned by a sixth sense, a vivid instinct that more than once had saved him from death, that was developed from his wild existence and the extreme danger he was in so much of the time, he whirled as clawing fingers dug into his left arm.

CHAPTER III
SLAVES

"Don't shoot, Jim!"

The fierce movement of the Ranger, the great strength of his rippling muscles, startled the hombre who had caught him. It was the man with the scar on his cheek and he gasped as he fell back under the sharp jab of the Ranger's Colt muzzle, rammed into his belly.

A sleeper roused and growled, "What the hell's that?"

Scarface's reply determined his fate. He said, "Aw, go back to sleep. It's jest Torquila bringin' up another gang."

Torquila! Captain McDowell had mentioned the Mex bandit who was taking advantage of the existing upset, to strike the Maravilla ranches and settlements, raiding as he pleased. And here Torquila was connecting with the Lumber Company!

Still wary, still ready to blast his way out of there, Hatfield pretended to relax. "Who's out there?" he demanded.

"Sh, quiet," whispered Scarface. "Put up yore gun, Jim old boy. I know yuh're only curious, but fer Gawd's sake don't let nobody else ketch you snoopin'. Ross'd soon kill you as not; he's okay but if he even smells spy he'll finish you. Git back to bed."

"Awright," drawled Hatfield. "But I got to watch my hide, pard. I ain't lettin' a posse slip up on me, savvy?"

Scarface sighed with relief, and Hatfield wondered if his new pal were as unsuspecting as he seemed. Hatfield lay down and Scarface did, too.

"I better work while I got the chance," the Ranger mused, as he lay with head in clasped hands. He was eager to make use of every instant in the enemy camp, aware Valentine Ross was not the sort to be fooled long. The cold-faced boss of the lumbermen must have an extraordinarily keen mind; Hatfield knew how tough and unruly lumberjacks were and that the dudish, skinny Ross could maintain himself over them only by a tiger ferocity, an extra-sharp mental equipment.

He stared at the small rectangle of the window, faintly red from the fire by the office. Then, against the frame, he caught a dark, roundish object slowly rising, that stayed only an instant and then ducked down. It was the top of a man's capped head. Someone was standing guard out there.

"Ross *is* suspicious," Hatfield decided. "Checkin' me, shore as hell's hot!"

The sentry must have heard some of the low-voiced talk between Hatfield and Scarface; it did not matter how much. He would have seen the Ranger's outline in the window. It changed the aspect of the situation; every instinct warned Hatfield. Ross had a couple of hundred armed men around to say nothing of Torquila's army.

The heavy breathing of the 'jacks in his ears, the odor of their sweated bodies in his flared nostrils, he watched the window for the guard. After a while he came up on his elbow and eased his booted feet to the dirt. "Hey, Scarface!" he whispered.

No answer. The tall man rose, a wraith in the darkness, tiptoed to the lean hombre's bunk. Scarface was asleep.

The window was too small to let him through. He pulled a .45 cartridge from a loop in his belt and tossed it out of the little opening so it clinked on the sill and rolled on the ground outside. With a panther's movements he reached the door; it creaked on its leather hinges as he pulled it open.

Now the space around the office seemed deserted. The bandits and Ross's men had herded their captives off through the trees. Hatfield looked back at the window and, as he had counted, the noise the cartridge had made had drawn the sentry to the window, giving the Ranger a few moments to get out the door.

Timing his exit perfectly, he closed the door and slid around the far end of the shack, and down the west side. Pausing at the southwest corner he peered along the south end. The guard was back at the southeast corner, watching the door, after he had investigated the sound Hatfield caused at the window.

"Like to have a look-see at that office," he mused, calculating his play. So far the only hitch was the sentry, the others having gone over to the compound.

The Ranger started, one foot after the other, feeling the dirt. He was within a yard of the crouched man, a hulking 'jack in corduroy and round cap, whose rifle leaned against the hut wall, before the guard heard him. The man swung with a gasped curse.

"What the — !"

The Ranger launched his powerful body through the intervening space. He glimpsed the 'jack's bearded, openmouthed face as his steel hand closed like a vise on the hairy throat. The fellow was strong, a fighter, hard as nails, but the Ranger's terrific attack knocked him back against the chinked logs; his cry was choked off by the long, inexorable fingers.

The man lashed out with a fist, hit the Ranger in the face, but the impetus of the officer's lunge was not checked. Hatfield drove a knee into the lumberman's belly and a dull crack sounded as the Ranger laid a heavy Colt barrel on the guard's head. It took all the fight out of the 'jack; buffaloed, he went limp, and Hatfield dragged him into the bush and flitted toward the office.

A lantern burned inside. The clearing fire was low; beyond stood a bunch of ponies, and there were saddled mustangs near, mounts kept ready by Ross and his crew. Coming up in the end shadow, Hatfield made sure he could duck into the hut unobserved; and then he was in. The lantern flickered on a table made of rough-cut sticks and an oak slab. His swift eyes took in the hanging clothes, the single bunk, and a brown suitcase pushed under it.

"Figger that forester snooped round here," he decided, "and didn't get far with Ross."

His slitted glance quickly discarded most of the furnishings. He came to the bunk, pulled out the suitcase. On one knee, a Colt laid beside him, he went through the contents. Some shirts and toilet articles. Then he found a small black notebook with a dried brown stain on its cover.

"Blood," he muttered. And inside the leaves was a silver badge marked, "STATE OF TEXAS. FOREST SERVICE."

"That's it," he said aloud, and opened the report book. Hasty scrawls showed on the first pages: "Ran into SW. L. Co.'s camp. Ross, the boss, gave me a job when I said I was after work. Showed me State lease to cut timber." Next: "These men are killers! Some real 'jacks but they're in cahoots. Cutting fortune in live-oak and pine, no heed for future growth. Must get evidence."

There wasn't any more. "Ross caught him huntin' that evidence," thought Hatfield, shoving the badge and book into a capacious hip pocket. "Wonder why Ross saved these?"

There were papers that intrigued him at the bottom of the bag. A lease from the State to cut timber, signed by the governor, and he found a large sheet that puzzled him, for he stared at it for some moments, vertical creases in his bronzed brow. It was, he concluded, a rough, hand-drawn map of central and south Texas, two wide lines run-

44

ning north and south that cut a great swathe in the outline of the state, reaching across the Rio Grande into Mexico. Yes, there was the Maravilla River, an uneven line from west to east. And small letters dotted about with no apparent system: "T", "C" right under it at the spot where stood the mountains he was in. Farther north, an "O" and to the west another "C" and two "I's".

"Now what the —" he muttered, and staring at it, suddenly he threw the papers back into the bag, grabbed up his gun and jumped over to the door.

He was cut off. Right on the office were Ross, Bigjaw Haley, Torquila and the mob of armed 'jacks and bandits.

Caught, Hatfield crouched to the side, back so he could not be seen unless someone actually stepped into the shack. He had a flash of Ross as the boss hustled, not into the office, but on past it. On Ross's flank strode the giant Torquila, and Hatfield glimpsed the cruel bearded face, dark as an Indian's, the cape flowing out in the speed of his movements. They headed, the whole bunch, to the hut where Hatfield supposedly slept, and gunmen ringed it. Ross, a lantern raised, kicked in the door.

"Rouse up, you big jigger!" he bawled.

45

The Ranger slipped outside, swung to the south end of the office, toward the bush. "He's gone!" Ross yelled. "Spy, spy!"

Starting away, Hatfield bumped into two lumberjacks hurrying from the stockade. They wore corduroy, roundish caps pulled low and heavy hobnail boots.

"Hey," demanded one, "where you goin'?"

"Tim!" cried the other, "it's the guy they figger's a spy!" And he bawled, "Ross, Ross, here he is!"

Both went for their guns. Hatfield's Colt flashed with the speed of legerdemain, hammer back under thumb. Tim, weapon coming to shooting level, crashed with a slug in the thigh, his bullet driving into the dirt between the Ranger's spread feet. The second let go and Hatfield, swinging his gun, felt lead burn his ribs. Then his firing-pin hit again and the 'jack whirled, clutching his punctured throat as he lost all volition, to fall across the writhing body of his pal.

Loud shouts rose as the whole camp roused and started for the Ranger.

Hatfield headed for the saddled horses on the other side of the fire. As he passed through the ruby light circle they saw him and a howl of hate rose. Blasting guns crashed in the scented night air and he heard slugs spitting in the leaves and needles, thuds as they hit tree-trunks or spurted up dirt. One bit a chunk from his boot, then he was among the mustangs, the animals dancing with alarm at the gunfire.

The Lone Wolf grabbed a fast looking black, vaulted into the saddle, slammed a fist down between the laid-back ears as the unruly beast reared and, knocking the horse into running position, lined out south through the forest. He preferred not to call Goldy into that death hail; the seconds delay in bringing up the golden flash would have meant destruction for both Goldy and the Ranger.

The bank of heavy guns, furious howls of the enemy followed him as he zigzagged south through the woods. He urged the black on by a low crooning. The creature recognized the masterful but friendly sound so that he calmed enough to give his best. The cries of hatred made a horrid din as the pack mounted to tear after the spy.

Hatfield cut down a slope carpeted by pine needles, cut up by rock formations. The going was shadowed, almost blind. Here and there moon rays like silver streams penetrated the trees; an owl hooted eerily near at hand, as he swung in his saddle to empty a Colt back at the mob.

"Jest as well I left that sleepin' hut," he mused, his nerves unshaken by the narrow squeak. Yes, Valentine Ross had suspected him, must have mentioned his distrust of the tall stranger to Torquila and they had come to investigate. They would have killed him had he not consented to a thorough search and questioning; they would have found his Ranger star, snugged in its secret pocket.

The mob was in full hue-and-cry on his trail; he headed the big black on south, crossed the swift Maravilla, and came onto a trail leading toward Old Mexico, sixty miles away. He rode with a masterful recklessness unmatched by other horsemen, the wind whistling past his ears. The mustang, once realizing the power of the rider, drove on at a breakneck speed.

Hatfield heard the leaders pounding behind, some hundreds of yards in his rear. He looked back. "Wonder how long they'll keep a-comin'?" he mused. "It'd be handy if I was back at the camp, with most of 'em gone."

Icy daring allowed the Lone Wolf to weigh such an angle, at such a moment. He would try, and he slowed her rounding the next turn. Choosing a spot where a stony formation hid rocks he swung the black up the steep bank into the trees.

Back in the deep shadows he dismounted, stood by the mustang's head with a hand over the beast's quivering nostrils. The leaders of the hunters swung into sight, he saw their heads and shoulders as they rode in the trail gully.

Torquila was among the first, great figure with cape sweeping back in the wind of speed. His bandits bunched on his heels, all wild, crazy riders; the lumberjacks, not so good in the saddle, straggled along. After a few minutes he apparently had passed.

The ground close around Hatfield was too cut-up to ride on; he led the pack to the trail, mounted and galloped back toward the Southwest's camp.

In the firelight he saw that only a few men had stayed behind. There was a way open among the trees; in the far distance north was the office and shacks. After crossing the Maravilla, Hatfield swung toward the stockade, the black walking through a forest lane.

Fluffy bits of white clouds swiftly swept across the face of the moon, dotting the earth with passing shadows; the sky was milky with stars, and the sweet west wind softly brushed the stern, rugged face of the tall Ranger, intent on his duty. The Maravilla gurgled innocently over its stony bed as though determined to deliver its sustenance to the people who depended upon it.

He came near the enclosure, dismounted and left the black with reins dragging, crept in foot by foot toward the stockade. From what he had observed he concluded the law of Texas was being flouted, beyond the killings and violence laid at the feet of the Lumber Company. It was big, bigger than it had sounded, and Jim Hatfield was not the sort to miss such a clue. Alone against a multitude, the Ranger meant to ferret out every crooked angle of the situation.

Crouched in the dense bush shadows, Hatfield watched the armed men slowly patrolling the square walls of the palisades. Downwind, he caught the stench from the corral, the fetid odor of uncared-for humanity, like the hold of a slave-ship. His eyes turned dark with rage; he could guess the treatment suffered by the unfortunate workers at the hands of the Southwest Lumber Company.

Behind Ross were other criminals, he had concluded from his swift survey. "Want to know who wangled that State concession to cut this timber. And how come we was so late gettin' word of all this. Now what's that funny map with all those letters mean?"

Someone had delayed reports on the

50

feverish activities of the Southwest, so they had had a free hand for some time before Austin was aware of what went on.

Every instant lessened the Ranger's chances of escaping with his life. Enemies seethed about him, eager to kill. His run had branded him a spy, there was no explaining now; it was cinched. But through his trick of rescuing Scarface he had gained valuable information, though Vasco Torquila had been quick enough to demand a full investigation of the big man posing as an outlaw.

"Smart Mex," mused Hatfield. "Hafta see him again."

Flat on his belly in the fringe of bush outside the stockade clearing, he heard moans of sick men; some were praying, others cursing. The high, rough poles of the palisade stuck fifteen feet into the air, barbed wire strung along the top. Barred gates faced him at the south where lounged half a dozen 'jacks, pistols in open-flapped holsters, rifles across their knees. He could hear them talking.

"Oh, they'll ketch him all right," one was saying. "Scarface got fooled, but not Ross, no sir. Betcha that bronc buster Morton sent him up to spy on us. By this time tomorrow we'll be fryin' that bronc buster's liver and we'll add that big jigger's."

"Yeah, that Morton's caused us plenty trouble," another 'jack growled. "I mean to take a crack at him myself. Why, when them cowboys ambushed us on the road the other day I nearly got shot! That was Morton's idee and he was the one that telegraphed Austin. He done it hisself, so there was no chanct to stop it."

Hatfield listened, ticketing every bit of information. But he could not linger; he had but a few minutes in which to act, and he crept around to the north, where he saw the black shapes of rocks sticking up close to the middle of the poles. A sentry, moonlight gleaming on metal Winchester barrel, came slowly along past the rocks, and paused for a word with his mate at the corner before swinging to stride back.

The Ranger saw the wholesale crime. He must check up on it and meant to do so while he could. He came erect as the sentry again passed along his side, swung with his back to the Ranger for a few moments. Seizing the opportunity, Hatfield scuttled across the narrow strip of moonlit open space, and ducked down between the rocks and poles before the guard turned to come along once more. The sentry passed Hatfield's hiding-place; he was almost entirely hidden in the black space. As soon as the 'jack was a few yards off, Hatfield put his lips to a space where two of the strong pine poles were wired together, and in a sibilant whisper, spoke in Spanish.

"Juan, Juan. Juan, Juan!" He expected, by use of this common Mexican name, to get a reply.

"Si, I'm here," a weak voice answered.

"You're Juan from — ?"

The Mexican peon groaned, "Juan Gonzales from Avalo. Help us, we're sick, dying!"

The peons close inside were rousing, growing excited; voices quivering with hope chattered eager questions.

"Sh! Quiet!" warned the Ranger, but the guard, swinging back, heard the sounds, and uttered a warning shout that echoed through the woods. He ran toward the spot where Hatfield crouched in the rocks.

"Hey, what's goin' on inside there?" he bawled.

The bunch up front had heard the alarm and were running in answer to the sentry's call. The guards along the other sides, too, were bearing down on Hatfield from either flank. The Ranger came up on his knees, opened fire as the nearest 'jack threw up his Winchester. The long rifle slug smacked the rock, the flaming flare stabbing the Ranger's

53

eyes; spattered fragments of stone cut his skin. But the steady Colt muzzle did not move as the Ranger raised thumb off hammer.

The 'jack threw up both hands, rifle flying off to thud on the dirt. Hatfield swung right, the acrid smell of burnt powder in flared nostrils, the glint of the fighting man shining in his slitted eyes.

He laid three .45 slugs into the oncoming enemy, dropped the hombre from the right before he could shoot. A third, close on him, let out a shriek as he saw his mates fall, and he went down on one knee, pumping bullets wildly at the rocks. Lead cracked the stone, one ripped the crown of Hatfield's Stetson as he rose up to run for the trees.

The main bunch was rounding the corner of the stockade. Hatfield emptied his Colt at the rifleman, sent him jumping back to his friends. He dropped his empty pistol into its holster and drew his second weapon. Hitting the trees he looked back, gun up. They sighted the dark, moving figure and whooped as they swung their muzzles on him.

Bullets hit the trunks of the pines, ripped the underbrush; Hatfield was cut off from the black mustang and he heard yells from the camp, knew Ross and Torquila were back.

Warm sweat of exertion rolled down his skin; he wiped it from his eyes for clear vision, and took a deep breath of the aromatic, cool air. He gave three shrill whistles, repeating them as he hustled west through the woods.

"There he goes! That way!" a lumberman shrieked.

The madness of murder burned them; a fury that drove them after the Ranger as a pack of hounds hunts down its quarry, hoping to tear him to pieces. And suddenly, before him, Hatfield saw the end of the covering woods.

Far as the eye could reach, bathed in the moonlight, stretched a scene of desolation. The silvered sky shone on miles cleared by the Southwest Lumber Company's greedy vandalism; bleeding, ragged tree stumps, blackened spaces where bush had been burned, the wreck of Nature's loveliness, hills and dales ripped open by the greed of man, mad for money. Piles of trimmed logs stood here and there, ready to be hauled away for sale.

He cut north, repeating his whistle; they were after him, and Ross, Torquila, most of the mob were mounted. One glimpsed him against the lighter space and bullets whirled about him. He swung to fire back, hold them.

Jim Hatfield, in his perilous work as a Texas Ranger, had been in many tight spots in his fight against the evil of those who sought power and wealth through unlawful means. He had ridden the Rio with Death as his mate; had seen the river run red with the blood of victims of Mexican raiders; had faced the Ghost Rider, and had run against the terrible power of city thieves who sought to pirate the rich oil lands of Alamita. He had fought against aroused Indians whose fury devastated the Border. But the Lone Wolf had never come closer to bloody death than when, with icy nerve and mad daring, he had ridden straight into the face of hundreds of hostile guns, commanded by the Southwest Lumber Company.

A hint of grayness was in the eastern sky; dawn, dawn that would make escape altogether impossible. Texas needed him, and Maravilla, bleeding from the awful thrusts of its powerful enemy, cried for his aid. He could not fail!

A shrill whinny sounded, and a golden ghost horse, saddle on, galloped up to him. Goldy had jumped the rope barrier holding him below the camp, had come in answer to his master's call.

"Good boy," muttered the Lone Wolf as he hit the saddle in a flying leap, and urged the sorrel north along the jagged line of the bleeding woods.

Under him, long legs locked in the familiar seat, the great sorrel paced off the yards in a businesslike gait. Nothing but a death bullet could stop Goldy now.

Hatfield lined the sorrel out, let Goldy have his head, as he ran before the howling army of killers who sought to take him and tear him to shreds for daring to interfere with their deadly plans.

CHAPTER IV
CAPTURED

Bancroft Morton had never been so happy as he was at the Bar W. Sanguine by nature, he was seldom downcast. Save for his intense love of horses little else had possessed him; an expert bronc buster is always in demand and he could find work when he wanted it, but his wanderings had been aimless. Now his life had a purpose.

Sam Ward lay, unable to move, in his old tester-bed, lovingly tended by Elsie. The chief of the Maravilla cowmen had not died; sore wounded, he was too tough to quit. Suffering, a bullet lodged close to his spine at one side, and too dangerous to be removed as yet, Ward could still smile at the soft-handed young woman who nursed him with such deep devotion. He could still command the ranchers who looked to him as leader.

Lately had ridden up young Ban Morton and Morton had proved his devotion to the cause. He had pointed out clearly the danger to the Maravilla range once the watershed was denuded, a strong point against the lumbermen. Aided by old Sam's shrewdness, Morton had figured out telling blows against the Southwest Lumber Company, such as sending waddies, armed with rifles, to harry at long range the mule and horse teams commanded by Bigjaw Haley.

Cut logs were being hauled to the railroad, and the wagons brought back liquor and food supplies on the return trip. The big outfits of the Maravilla had each contributed half a dozen riders who were ordered by Ward not to close with the enemy but to make it too hot for them to get through, blocking delivery of the timber. Hitting and running, they had forced Valentine Ross to hold back his output and even now the ranchers' band was lying to the north, watching for the lumbermen.

That morning, as Jim Hatfield was pursued by the infuriated army of Torquila and Ross, Morton left his bunk early as was his habit. He went out and washed at the pump, then strolled to the kitchen. Guards had been placed around the ranch, on Ban's advice, to prevent any surprise attack by the 'jacks on Sam Ward.

Through the night a ring of them rode in

the moonlight. The Bar W had fifty punchers, all tough fighters. The night guards were now coming in, to get some food and sleep; the day punchers were rising. Elsie was up. Her face was drawn and Ban Morton was saddened to see the terrible strain she was undergoing but she smiled on him and gave him a pert little nod that touched him with its sheer courage.

At her invitation he helped himself to coffee, fried potatoes, bacon and biscuits left by the cook on the lean-to stove, and she sat down with him while he ate. She brushed back a wisp of dark hair that had strayed over her long-lashed blue eyes; dainty of body as she was she had exhibited a marvelous strength in the ordeal that had come upon them.

"We jest can't let them 'jacks cut any more of that timber, Elsie," said Ban. "They've ruint miles of the watershed awready. Yuh saw in the cloudburst the other day how roiled the river got; even 'fore the tree roots rot out a heavy downpour'll wash off the topsoil."

She sighed. "It's awful, Ban. But what can we do, till we get more help? They've so many men up there and they seem to know every move we make."

Morton took a gulp of the warm, brown

coffee. The familiar kitchen odor, the joy he felt in Elsie's company and her trust, thrilled him with a deep content. He was eager to help the ranchers.

The injury to their chief, Ward, was a serious blow from which they were just recovering. Demoralized by the disastrous defeat that day, they had taken little action since. The bold raids of Vasco Torquila kept the Vigilantes skipping from spot to spot, and the ranch owner dared not leave his home with too small a guard for the fear the giant bandit would strike.

"I figger we ought to drive every steer we kin round up away from the west sections, Elsie," Ban Morton told her. "That'll make it harder for them dawgs to rustle 'em, anyway."

"Let's ask Father," she suggested.

When he was through eating, Elsie led Ban Morton through the cool, rambling house to the side bedroom where Sam Ward lay in the old-fashioned mahogany bed carted out from Missouri when he had first come to the Maravilla. Ward, a wadding of bandage on his wound, lay on his side, stiff and uncomfortable. He listened to Ban's idea and nodded.

"Tell Nevada to start this mornin'. Morton, we got to save Maravilla. Now I've thought it over I see I was foolish to go off half-cocked the way I did; I jest led my friends into a death trap. I should've organized more keerful. Sheriff Godey's comin' down this afternoon, and I reckon the Rangers'll be here pronto. Then we'll act."

"It wasn't yore fault," Ban told him, seeing Ward's inward distress, that he blamed himself for the fiasco. "Anybody would've done the same. I'll help with the drive today."

He nodded and went out into the hall, and Elsie following him, touched his arm. "Be mighty wary, Ban. If they catch you they'll kill you. That bullet that went through your hat the other night makes it plain."

"Yeah, it's a cinch somebody don't like me hornin' in here. But I'm safe enough on Black Rascal."

She was standing close to him, and the words they spoke were calm and emotionless; yet, behind the matter-of-fact speech their hearts spoke. Elsie looked up into his youthful, pleasant face. And Ban Morton was overcome by an emotion he could not resist; he seized her and kissed her, and she put her arms around his neck.

"Elsie — I love yuh," he whispered.

"I love you, Ban dear. You've been wonderful."

Someone cleared his throat behind them, engrossed as they were in one another. Ban Morton swung, saw a lean, saturnine hombre, Nevada Lewis, standing on the long veranda; Lewis had seen them kissing through the open door.

" 'Mornin'," Nevada drawled. "Jest comin' for orders."

Ban Morton frowned. He was rattled, caught that way kissing his girl, and he didn't like Lewis much. Nevada spoke very little and seemed to resent Morton's presence at the Bar W, for Ban had usurped the foreman's natural rôle as Ward's favorite.

"Orders're to run in all the cows from the west range," growled Morton.

Nevada Lewis nodded. Elsie went back into her father's room and Ban, with his stiff-legged gait, strolled out. He went to the round corral where ranch horses were kept for use at night, and roped a hard-mouthed buckskin, a fast horse but a bad actor, that he was gradually gentling. Black Rascal he had turned out in a grass pasture down by the Maravilla and like most cowboys Morton never walked any distance if he could ride.

Reaching the pasture, a large enclosure on

the river, it was some minutes before he looked over the two hundred mustangs inside and realized his pet was missing.

At first he was not alarmed; maybe some hurried nighthawk had roped Black Rascal. He rode back to the corrals and looked in the barns, but the handsome horse wasn't there, either. Nevada Lewis was standing outside the bunkhouse, and Morton limped up to him, as the foreman doused his whole head in a bucket of cold water.

"Seen my hoss?" Ban demanded.

Nevada slowly dried his dripping face and hair with the community towel before he spoke. "Why, no," he drawled. "He missin'?"

"Yeah. And the man who took him will never steal another," Ban slowly declared.

The foreman shrugged. A calf bawled in the distance; mustangs stamped in the pens. Punchers were up, to a new day of toil on the range. The familiar sounds of the ranch were in Morton's ears as he swung, heart grieving at Black Rascal's disappearance. He kept hoping his pet would gallop up, as he went around asking various men if they had seen him. No one had.

The pasture was not far from the house and guards had been out all night, but the nighthawks lay in close to the buildings and a clever thief could have slipped through.

As Morton went to mount the buckskin, riders appeared from the east, dust rising under the clipping hoofs of their animals. He waited.

John Ogalvie of the Circle 5, east of Bowietown, George Keith of the Running R, to the north, and Mayor Yager galloped up. Ban knew them all, leaders of Maravilla, able lieutenants of Ward.

"Howdy, Ban," sang out the hearty mayor, grinning at the slim bronc buster. "How's Sam today?"

" 'Bout the same and still chipper," replied Ban. He liked the big mayor who always had a kind word for everybody.

They dismounted in front of the house, and Yager slapped Ban on the back. "We're goin' to hit them lumbermen snakes and pronto, no fooling," growled Yager. "Come to talk it over with Sam."

Ban trailed them into Ward's room. After greetings were over Yager said, "Sam, we're collectin' every fighting man in Maravilla. We could muster four hundred, arm 'em, and attack those devils and drive 'em out pronto."

To their obvious surprise, Ward shook his head. "They're too strong set up there, Smiley. We sorta got 'em cinched for a while and I'd rather wait'll the Rangers get here and make shore there's no mistake like before."

Ogalvie looked at Yager, and the mayor scratched his head. They were, Ban Morton decided, rather dashed at Ward's lack of enthusiasm for their plan. And some doubt, too; Morton thought they might be wondering if his injury had broken the big rancher chief.

"I'd like to get my hands on them," growled Yager.

"Well, Sam," John Ogalvie said slowly, "I still think we could wipe 'em off the map but —" He shrugged. Keith nodded; these men were the sort who would be loyal to the death.

Ban Morton was restless; he couldn't forget Black Rascal. "Gotta find him," he muttered.

"Godey's comin' today," Ward said, "and I'm hopin' the Rangers'll soon be down. Then we'll hit."

Morton slipped away from the conference and mounted the buckskin, straightened the unruly beast out, and rode over to the pasture. To his surprise Nevada Lewis rode up to join him as he was casting around.

"That's a fine hoss of yores," Lewis growled. "Don't blame yuh for worryin'." He began to help Ban hunt for traces.

The dirt was cut up by countless hoofs but Nevada, riding a widening circle, ran on some fresh prints a few hundred yards west, close to the river bank.

"How 'bout these?" he sang out.

Ban trotted the buckskin over and got down. Black Rascal had a groove in his left front shoe and sure enough there was a mark like that in the soft spot.

"Led by two men," remarked Morton. "One on a white with a throwout to his left hind laig." There was a white horsehair, and the hoofprint told him the animal's idiosyncrasy.

"Want me to ride with yuh?" asked Lewis.

Morton shook his head. The foreman had work to do and Ban wanted to follow that trail alone. Nevada nodded and swung back.

Ban Morton shoved the buckskin west, eyes on the rising hills with their stands of live-oak and pine. His keen vision made out the line of that great ditch, here and there where the foliage did not obscure the view. As he drew nearer he glimpsed toiling ants he knew were hundreds of peon laborers, working on the ditch.

"In a hurry to get it through," he muttered, "but they can never use it with us hamperin' 'em. They must know that."

Cows ranged the grassy, well-watered sections. The land was lovely, with greens and browns, and the star-white blossoms of the high mesquite, here and there a sandy cactus flat where flourished giant ocotillos, and prickly pear with green-and-purple fruit. Lines of stones had caught the wind-wafted seeds of granjeno and the bushes grew in dense hedges, like walls.

Feathery huisache trees turned their leaves to the gentle wind; a road-runner scampered from the man's path; the whir of a giant rattlesnake sounded and the buckskin nervously jumped aside. The odors were sweet, and mixed with the rich damp earth and grass smell and the aromatic odors of creosote and sage. Crows cawed on his flanks; a bunch of cows threw up their tails and thundered off at sight of him. The sky was a deep blue dome where burned the brilliant golden ball of the sun.

The Maravilla was a gorgeous land, a happy home. But over it hung the gigantic, clutching greed of man. Terror was smashing that happiness, destroying the people of Maravilla; like a swift-growing cancer, threatening to spread throughout mighty Texas.

Morton swung northwest, meaning to come up from that side; he was on guard, ready for trouble with the lumberjacks. Suddenly a rider darted out from a wall of thorny granjeno, off to Ban Morton's left. He let go with a pistol and Morton heard the whistle of the bullet past his head. The man ahead was on a big white and Morton noted the outflung left hind leg, even as he saw the shiny black horse led by a rope behind.

"Black Rascal!" he cried. Morton forgot caution at sight of his pet; he dug in his spurs and lined the buckskin out in mad pursuit.

For a mile they flew on. Morton was gaining. The going was uphill, rocky in places, and the bush thicker and wilder. Morton fired several times, but dared not aim too close for fear of hitting Black Rascal. The horse-thief now and then would swing and send back a bullet but the jolting speed of the chase prevented careful aim.

Morton galloped right into the trap. The buckskin, traveling full speed, hell-for-leather, was violently swirled around, neck giving a sharp crack as lariats settled over him, thrown from the bushed sides of the draw. Hidden men had tossed those deadly nooses, with unerring skill; while two roped the buckskin, bringing him around, falling, others circled the bronc buster, who was exerting every ounce of skill to maintain his seat at the buckskin's mad jerk.

The buckskin went down and Morton hit the ground running. The lariats tightened, pulled him down, too, with a thud, and, wind knocked out of him, he found his arms completely helpless because of the binding ropes.

Men in peaked hats, leather chaps, some barefoot with spurs tied to their ankles, who wore crossed ammunition belts over khaki military jackets; swarthy of face, dark of eye, ran upon him, yelling in triumph. Vaqueros turned bandit, they could throw a reata with deadly skill. A bunch of them fell on Morton before he could wriggle out of the loops. He was kicked, goaded with needle spurs; they cursed him in Mexican, laughing at his anger, at his attempts to fight back.

He knew he had, through his deep love for Black Rascal, run into this death trap. They tied his wrists and legs, threw him across Black Rascal's back like a sack of flour, and headed north for the lumber camp. And well up toward the hills a man with a bear's wide, powerful body, reddish of hair and beard, clad in dirty corduroy, bullwhip under his arm, met them.

"Got him, huh?" growled Bigjaw Haley. "Nice work, boys. The boss'll be glad to see this polecat." He lurched to the helpless

Morton, fierce, red-rimmed eyes glaring into the bronc buster's face.

Ban Morton set his teeth, determined not to let them see he was suffering. His look evidently angered Haley for Bigjaw snatched his whip and slashed Morton's body with the lead-tipped lash. A wave of red agony swept Ban. Black Rascal reared and snorted wildly.

"C'mon, bring him along," order Bigjaw.

Morton glimpsed the workers at the deep ditch; they were driven by brute overseers, mule-skinners assigned to this job, for Morton's plan prevented them from delivering their timber now. The workmen were Mexicans, ragged, the misery of death in liquid Latin eyes. Thin and peaked, goaded without mercy, they dug into the red clay. Hundreds of horses and mules drew rough scoops or wagons of dirt, banking the sides.

But Ban Morton had little chance to observe the activity. They crossed on a rough bridge of logs roped together by rawhide and started on up the wooded slopes. Bigjaw Haley led; a dozen Mexican bandidos surrounded the prisoner.

"You ain't got long to live," railed Haley, spitting a brown tobacco stream from his rusty-bearded lips. "Once the chief gits his hands on you you'll wish you never was born. You'll be glad to die."

Morton hid his fear, held himself with a tight rein. Hope was gone; they would kill him, evidently after some torture, promised by Bigjaw Haley.

"What's the idee?" he demanded.

"Why, whippersnapper," said Haley meaningly, "we'll larn you not to fool with real men. You've horned in on our game and you got too many cute idees. Besides, the chief don't like you personally."

Only one very thin chance remained; when they turned him loose he would run or maybe snatch a gun and shoot a way out. It was awful to die, now he had found life's purpose; he kept thinking of Elsie, and sternly told himself not to be a fool; he'd go soft if he dwelt on that . . .

The lurching of Black Rascal as he plodded up the rocky slopes toward the Southwest Lumber Company's main camp, hurt Morton's ribs and belly. But he was sure the hastily wrapped ropes on his legs were also loosening under the strain and he kept expanding and contracting his calf muscles, cords biting the flesh. "If I could get that loose," he thought agonizedly.

He kept working at the leg bindings, pulling one leg up a little, then down, movements hidden by the motion of Black Rascal; after a while the tighter loops slipped and he figured he could pull his feet out of his boots and so be able to run.

"Hey, mister," he groaned, feigning deep distress, "lemme down. I gotta rest. I'm dizzy as hell."

Bigjaw Haley just laughed, spat tobacco juice.

"You'll be a sight dizzier tonight," he promised.

Ban Morton closed his eyes, let his head go limp, as though fainting. Through lowered lashes he saw a rock pile to the north, fringed by heavy granjeno bushes. Maybe, once on his feet, he could dive through behind the stones, for cover to run.

When Black Rascal gave a lurch that way Morton slid off the horse's back, as though senseless. He hit the ground, and as the following bandits swerved their shaggy mounts to avoid colliding with Black Rascal who had naturally stopped when his rider fell, Morton kicked off the loops and leaped up.

He dived head first for the thorny bushes, that scratched his skin; his hands were still tied behind. His quick act caught them off guard, but as Morton came up on his knees in an effort to get around behind the rocks, where he would stand a chance of running, Bigjaw Haley swung his long lash, spurring his horse, at Morton.

The leaded tippets viciously wrapped around Ban's throat and head, biting into his cheeks he was violently jerked backward, and fell on his side. The whip came free and Haley struck again, across the back of Morton's head. With a howl of rage Haley leaped down and began to lash Ban across the back.

A red miasma of pain, pain too great to bear, engulfed Ban Morton. Merciful darkness hit him and he lay quiet as the burly muleskinner tore into him, ripping his clothes off with terrible blows of the lash.

"The chief kin have what's left," yelled Bigjaw.

CHAPTER V
THE OTHER SIDE

"Well," mused Ranger Jim Hatfield, "it worked once — why not now?"

He raised his Colt, and took aim.

After shaking off his pursuers early that morning he had spent some time hidden in the dense bush north of the Lumber Company's camp. He had slept a few hours to make up for the lost night.

Having observed the devastation of the Ord Mountains and hills to the west through which the Southwest Company had cut, noted from a height the rough, winding trail they had formerly used to cart the timber north to the Southern Pacific at Lenox, he had started east for the Bar W and Bowie, to organize efficient resistance and ferret out several mysteries which he had come upon. There was that map with the fine lettering; the stoppage of the messages to Austin; the peon workers, brought in from Mexico by Vasco Torquila, a very important angle.

Hatfield knew he was bucking an extremely powerful combine, that could command a multitude of guns. He did not miss the activity on the east slopes, where the great ditch was being pushed through, and observed that it ran from close to the Maravilla toward a natural arroyo that led north for many miles.

"Not a bad idee," he decided. "Got to give 'em credit. Save a lot of time and tough haulin'. Draggin' them heavy trees across cut-up hills ain't easy. Only the rancher'll stop 'em."

Far-off shots attracted him and from a commanding bluff he had looked down on the capture of Ban Morton. He recognized Bigjaw Haley and the semi-military figures of the bandits, and he guessed their victim was a member of the opposition. Then the gray-green, shaded eyes narrowed, as he recalled the words he had overheard concerning a young bronc buster named Morton.

"Callate they've got him," he muttered. He had meant to stop at the Bar W and warn this Morton.

"If I pick him away from them, it oughta give me a quick introduction to the ranchers. 'Sides, from the way Haley acts, he'll be killed shore."

It had taken him some time to work down where he could cut their trail as they climbed into the hills. He left Goldy back a way in the bush and hustled up behind the rock pile, where Morton made his attempt to escape.

The Ranger had gained a lot by snatching Scarface from the cowboys; he expected to gain again by saving this decent looking young fellow from Haley, who was lashing him to death. The Maravilla people would be suspicious of a stranger till he proved himself, and Hatfield, not wishing as yet to announce himself a Ranger, knew he must act swiftly, for Texas. Thinking over that queer map he had seen in Ross's suitcase had given Hatfield a hunch. Perhaps the men behind the Southwest Lumber Company might have more than local plans.

Bigjaw Haley had his thick right arm raised, the bullwhip snapping overhead, as Hatfield drew a steady bead and put a bullet through the center of the wide wrist. Haley screamed as the smashed tendons let go and the whip flew from his unnerved fingers.

The shot, with its echoing report, electrified the bandit gang. With shrill yells they unshipped their guns to fight. Hatfield, Stetson down to his gray-green eyes, the crown just showing over the top of a flat boulder, blasted the bunch of them with his bullets, and two men fell off their mustangs.

The rest began shooting at him, but he had good cover and they were in the open. He picked off a third as they tried to stand; the survivors, appalled at the sudden slaughter and the screams of wounded, swung their hairy ponies, dug deep with spurs, and rode off into the south bush.

Bigjaw Haley, dazed, sat down hard, holding his bleeding, stubby wrist. His bearded jaw sagged, brown saliva dripping from gaping lips. Hatfield, Colt up, vaulted the boulder and slid down the slope to the prostrate figure of Ban Morton.

Haley stared wide-eyed at the tall figure of the Ranger, whose gun emitted a faint, uneven trickle of smoke. Fear flashed into the reddish eyes as they fixed on the great fighting man. Haley had never before realized he had nerves in his wide, stocky body, but he began to shake as though with ague, and a stifled screech welled in his hairy throat.

He groveled in the dirt, crying for mercy: "Don't kill me, mister. Don't!" He had never acted that way before, had considered himself too tough to crack. But he had seen this big jigger fight off the whole gang the night before, and get away with it. In addition, the torn tendons of his punctured wrist took all the strength out of him.

Hatfield paused an instant, staring at the strange sight of the broken muleskinner. "Next time, Haley, I'll kill yuh." It was a plain statement of fact and Haley believed it.

A bullet from a bandit, in ambush a hundred yards south, spanged on a stone a foot from Hatfield's big boot. He fired at the smoke spurt. He had to get Ban Morton out of there and, lifting Morton, he tossed him across the big black horse who stood quietly, nosing his master. He grabbed Black Rascal's bridle and led him around the rocks into the thick bush.

Haley began crawling for cover. The bandits, seeing Hatfield retreat, regained heart and came riding back, shooting into the mesquite, madly yelling.

Down behind a granite boulder, safe from the big jigger, Bigjaw Haley regained his aplomb. "Get him, get that feller," he howled, but he did not show any part of himself.

Hatfield quickly yanked Black Rascal to the spot where Goldy, the magnificent sorrel, waited. The Mexicans were coming through after him, but they had to dismount and lead their ponies for some yards before remounting, the ground too rough to ride.

A lariat still dangled from Black Rascal's saddle horn, the one used in tying Ban. Hatfield took a few turns to secure the unconscious man. This delay, and reloading his Colts, allowed the bandidos to come up. He heard them in the bushes and leaped at them, both guns blaring. A man shrieked a Spanish oath; slugs ripped around Hatfield as he crouched, throwing lead at the enemy. His bold stand routed them again, and they fell back.

Hatfield jumped to Goldy, mounted the golden sorrel, who was impatiently stamping, and started east out of the hills. The growth was thick, and the ground uneven, and at his heels like a pack of raging dogs came the remnants of the bandits, harrying him at a distance for they feared his deadly guns.

The lovely face of Nature, the green of the trees, the blossoms, yellow, red and white of the bush, and the pastel shades of the rock formations made an ironical setting for the fierce guerrilla fight that raged down the slopes. Gorgeous-hued butterflies flitted up from the flowers, the bees and ants pursued their busy tasks without taking note of the man-made hell close upon them. On all this, the sun smiled benignly, as though the fury of man did not exist.

The staccato bark of the guns echoed along the hillsides. A bullet bit a piece out of Hatfield's left arm; he bound a strip of his shirt around the wound without slowing, for he was aware he must get down across that ditch and on his way toward the ranches eastward before the lumberjacks organized pursuit. There were many of them off to the south, and they must have heard the shooting and Haley's powerful shouts.

A look at Black Rascal told him he was a super horse, capable of high speed; but Ban Morton was still out, unable to grip his saddle, and that meant the run would be slowed. Goldy kept sniffing, wishing to open up as they came to the arroyo, a deep dry ditch, in former times the Maravilla's bed, but now filled only during heavy rains. Some natural change had sent the river into its present course.

Dimly Hatfield heard yells off to the south, where the 'jacks and muleskinners lashed the peons on. Haley was heading toward his men, roaring orders at them. It would not be long until a howling army of killers would join the few bandidos.

It took time to ride along the arroyo, to

find a slide where he could cross the horses.

The slope beyond eased off but it was still slow going. The bandits kept screeching to mark the Ranger's position for the lumbermen, starting down to cut him off.

He calculated the remaining distance to the flats, where he could make better time. He would not leave Morton. Ahead lay rolling prairie, fairly open, where he could prevent them from ambushing him, at least.

The Ranger, the hope of Maravilla in this crisis, of Texas itself, for he alone guessed the extent of the raiders' plans, now was held back, and death was closing in, for he refused to think of dropping Ban Morton. If he died it would be defending the bronc buster. And, if he died, with him was lost all chance to stop the juggernaut of evil that was fast gaining momentum over Texas.

Not yet had he completely fathomed the plot of the enemy; he knew he must ride hard, ride fast and surely, to gather them all in. There was Avalo, in Old Mexico, near which must be Torquila's lair; there was the great valley of the Maravilla and the northern sections of the state. All of them marked by that wide swathe on the map.

He pushed on, Black Rascal following Goldy. He was but two hundred yards out on the grassy plain when a whole mob of 'jacks and muleskinners, armed with rifles and pistols, dashed from the bush and opened fire. Hatfield swung to send slugs back at the masses of men, to spoil their aim. Goldy was picking up speed on the level and Black Rascal, Morton perilously lurching with his motion, coming on with the sorrel.

The jolting stirred Ban Morton and he opened his eyes in his swollen face, streaked with clotted blood from the whip weals.

"What — ?" he muttered dizzily.

"Take it easy," the Ranger told him coolly. "Yuh're on yore way home, Morton."

For a time Morton did not speak; but he was coming fully awake, but on account of the ropes and his weakness he could not right himself on Black Rascal's back.

On the rolling stretches the renegades rode with the wild abandon of their race. They were far ahead of the slower moving lumbermen, yet Hatfield had thinned them out so only half a dozen stuck on his trail. Enemy bullets whirled in the air, plugged into the earth. A herd of cows snorted off in alarm at the gunfire, throwing up dust that clogged the forward vision, but as he rode through the cloud it helped protect him from his enemies.

"Look," the injured Morton called,

"there's s'posed to be a bunch of the boys workin' a few miles east of here today. They'll help us."

Hatfield nodded, grave eyes hunting back over his broad shoulder. They were drawing up and the Mexicans were threatening to cut him off as they opened out in a wide, circling movement.

CHAPTER VI
BOWIE

Hatfield's eyes hunted a spot where he could take cover to fight off the killers in a final stand, for they were coming up and the renegades were now shooting from both flanks. Then he saw dust to the north and turned toward it, guns blasting back the three Mexicans that way.

Twenty Bar W waddies were busy with a bunch of steers, running them out of reach of the lumberjacks. The arrival of the Ranger, the attackers on his heels, threw the herd into a stampede. Hatfield was met by a cursing foreman, a dark saturnine-faced hombre.

"What the hell's the idee, runnin' into my cows thisaway?" Nevada Lewis bawled.

"We brought you some company," Hatfield told him easily, meeting the hot eyes of the lean man.

Nevada saw Morton then. "Afternoon, Nevada," Ban drawled. "I'm back."

At sight of the enemy the Bar W men grabbed out their guns and started shooting. Howls of fury rose as the 'jacks, balked of their prey, stopped and lined up for battle. Nevada Lewis grunted, brows drawn tight together. He jerked a Colt and began firing at the lumbermen.

"Yuh're aimin' too high," Hatfield told him.

"I can stick in a saddle now, mister," Ban remarked.

Hatfield helped the injured bronc buster to sit up. Ban's face was twisted by pain. Hatfield decided to run him home. "Keep 'em busy," he said to Lewis. "We'll ride ahead."

Guns crackled in the warm air of afternoon, as Hatfield and Ban rode east, Morton pointing the way. The Bar W waddies slowly retreated, and the enemy, after a short scrap, stopped and turned back toward the hills. More armed men were near the ranch and they passed Morton and the Ranger, galloping to reinforce Nevada and his bunch.

"We keep guards out to protect Sam Ward," Morton explained. He told Hatfield the situation, fully trusting him after the Ranger's terrific feat against the enemy. The story of Black Rascal's strange disappearance interested the keen officer.

"Yuh say this Nevada helped yuh find them tracks?" asked Hatfield.

"Why, yeah. It was decent of him, seein' as how I've sorta took his place around the ranch."

It was, thought Hatfield, an interesting point. Remembering Scarface, who had connected with some other spy at the Bar W, he made a mental note to check Foreman Lewis.

Hatfield helped Ban dismount at the rear corral. Morton thought he'd lie in his bunk, but Elsie came running out and she cried when she saw her sweetheart's injured face.

"Ban, what's wrong?"

Ban managed to smile, through gritted teeth. "I'm okay, Elsie. This gent saved my life."

Hatfield regarded the pretty young woman, heiress to the Bar W. Her soft eyes were on the great Ranger's broad-shouldered figure, and she was plainly impressed by the stalwart fighting man, by his manner. The rugged face was calm as a summer sky, and though there was blood on him and he was torn from bullets and thorns, he was entirely unruffled.

Ban Morton, the strain over, suddenly collapsed. His knees buckled and his head went limp as Hatfield caught him.

"Oh bring him inside, quick," Elsie cried, terribly distressed.

The Ranger carried the young fellow easily, following Elsie to a bedroom near the center of the big house, where he deposited Morton on the cot. The Ranger told the worried young woman to bring him a drink and tie up his wounds and he'd be okay.

Morton opened his eyes, and swore after a moment. "Sorry," he muttered. "Didn't figger I'd do that."

Hatfield was rolling a cigarette; seeing Ban's look he gave it to Morton and fixed another, and Morton said awkwardly, "I'm obliged."

"Don't mention it." Hatfield understood that Ban Morton was thanking him, not for the cigarette but for what he had done. By future actions, Ban Morton showed his gratitude.

Elsie brought in a bottle of whiskey and after awhile Ban felt better and she returned to the kitchen to heat some water and fix bandages for his wounds. By a few casual queries, Hatfield drew out more of the rancher's story.

"Someone's after my hide," Ban Morton ended. "Ross and his pals're all-fired smart; they know ev'ry move we make."

"They were all ready the day Ward was shot, weren't they?" asked Hatfield.

"Yeah."

"Expectin' 'em," mused the Ranger, slouched in a chair, blue tobacco smoke wreathing his black-haired head. He turned the complicated business over in mind. "Callate I need to get it all straight, 'fore organizin'," he decided inwardly.

Both men were hungry and Elsie fed them. She said, "I'd like you to meet Father, Mr. — ?"

"Jim, Jim Harris," Hatfield told her gravely.

He followed the pretty girl across the wide living room to Sam Ward's chamber, where the giant rancher chief lay on his bed of pain. The Ranger's gray-green eyes fixed on the prostrate man, whose ruddy face was peaked by his ordeal. When Elsie told him what Hatfield had done, Ward smiled, straight-looking blue eyes ringed by lines of anguish. In a hoarse voice he thanked the Ranger.

"Ban's come to mean a lot to us, mister."

Riders, then, came sweeping into the yard. Steps on the porch and Elsie turned, with the Ranger, to see who was coming. Nevada Lewis, the foreman, dust-covered, dark face set, stood in the doorway, and behind him was a short hombre the Ranger immediately recognized. The waddy with Lewis was the man from whose hand Hatfield had shot a gun when the Ranger, heading in for Maravilla, had snatched Scarface from the lynch party.

Hatfield was alert, inwardly; but the short cowboy, filmed with sweat-caked dust, looked right at him and gave no sign of recognition; the Ranger had taken care to hide himself when he made that bold play, had even disguised his voice.

"What's wrong, Nevada?" Ward demanded.

A cigarette drooped from the pale lips of Lewis; for a moment his deep-sunk eyes fixed the Ranger, then swung to Ward. "Boss, somethin's went wrong with the river; it's most dried up, nuthin' but a trickle left. Shorty here jest rode in."

"They got the stream turned into that ditch, boss, and through the old arroyo," Shorty reported. "There's logs floatin' through, but they ain't tried to pick 'em up yet. They can't, not with us gunnin' 'em from the mesquite."

Ward was terribly perturbed. He licked his cracked lips, and Elsie held a glass of water to his mouth.

"That settles it," the old fellow gasped.

"We gotta go up after them sidewinders, like Haley said."

"Yore man's right," Hatfield put in. "The Southwest can't float logs to market with vigilantes pickin' 'em off."

"True," Ward agreed. "Only we can't last long 'thout the river. Stock'll die and people get sick. The Maravilla makes this country."

Hatfield knew that. He nodded, rose and went out. From the front veranda he could see the Maravilla; the sides were drying down from the banks, stones showing white and bare, like the bleached bones of a skeleton; in the center of the bed ran a brook, trickles from rills and springs below the spot where the Southwest Company had diverted the main stream. And, from the east, on the road winding along the river, riders were galloping toward the ranch.

The tall Lone Wolf lounged off to one side as this party swirled up, two dozen heavily armed men. They were plainly excited. All wore cowboy clothes save for a very tall, spare man in a black frock coat and straight black hat under which showed iron-gray, crisp hair; his gaunt face was triangular in shape.

"Like a beanpole all dressed up," the Ranger thought.

There was a man of about fifty, in riding

91

pants and black halfboots, Stetson and vest on which was pinned a five-pointed country sheriff's star; sharp-pointed goatee and ragged mustache salted with white. He took off his ten-gallon hat to mop with a red bandanna a head devoid of hair save for some curly fringes around his ears. Also there was a small oldster with a wooden peg-leg, wearing a town marshal's badge.

A bluff, square man with thick brown hair, sun-seamed eyes, sang out, "Oh, Elsie — where are you?"

Then he caught the Ranger regarding him and he took in the tall jigger, the bullet-ripped clothes, dried blood; suspicion darkened his broad face.

"Who are you?" he demanded.

All eyes swung on Hatfield. They were leary of strangers in Maravilla, and this stranger was obviously just out of a gunfight. Yet the Ranger's appearance awed men and no one made any move against him as he watched them with calm, calculating eyes, and Elsie Ward hurried out.

Only a half dozen, the leaders, of the bunch left their horses; the rest stayed outside, and they looked like armed waddies, followers of the chiefs of Maravilla.

"Hello, Senator and Mayor Yager. Hello, Johnny and all, Dad'll be happy to see you, come on in." Sensing the stiffness in the air she added quickly, "Oh, this is Jim Harris. He saved Ban Morton from death up in the hills; Ban was set on and almost killed by the lumbermen. Jim, meet Sheriff Godey, and this is Mayor Yager; Senator Ardmore, Marshal Betts. And John Ogalvie of the Circle 5, George Keith who owns the Running R, south of Bowie."

The tall senator cleared his bony throat. "We are obliged to Mr. Harris for saving Ban Morton," he announced sonorously.

Mayor Yager smiled at Elsie; but there was anxiety in his voice when he spoke.

"You know the river's gone. Means the country's ruined. We got to see your father, quick."

Senator Ardmore detached himself from the group, came to Hatfield. "Welcome to our fair land, sir. You've evidently had a long, hard ride and a bloody fight."

The Ranger knew he must quickly gain the confidence of the Maravilla ranchers. His saving of Morton had broken the ice, but he still had not explained his presence in the district.

"I'm a State Forester, Senator," he drawled. "Was up lookin' over them hills when I seen Morton set on."

Ardmore glanced over his shoulder, then

said delicately, "Perhaps you have some symbol of your authority, sir?"

"Shore." Without appearing offended, Hatfield drew forth the forester badge he had taken from Ross's suitcase. Mayor Yager's face broke into a smile at sight of that, and he came over, thrusting out a hearty hand.

"Glad to meet you, Harris. We can use you."

Tension eased; stiff suspicion faded, and, with the bluff mayor and others, Hatfield went back into the bedroom where lay Sam Ward.

"The river's gone, Sam, you know it," Yager growled.

"Now we got to fight, pronto," John Ogalvie added.

Ward nodded. "Figger yuh're right, boys." Ward looked sharply at Sheriff Godey down whose bearded face the sweat was running. "Godey, if you can't stop them devils, we can!"

"We'll send up every fightin' man in Maravilla," Mayor Yager cried. "Four hundred of 'em."

"Yeah," Ward agreed, "but this time they got to be armed right, and scouts out ahead, gents. It'll take two, three days to collect 'em and see they got plenty guns and bullets."

"Friday," Ogalvie suggested. "That'll give the outlyin' ranches time to get to Bowie from where we'll start."

"Right," Yager agreed, and Ward nodded.

"Some of Torquila's Mexes gunned us from across the river as we were comin' out," the mayor said. "That's another bunch of snakes we've got to wipe out, soon as we finish up on the Southwest, Sam. The law round here just can't seem to take care of us." He frowned at Godey again.

Godey again took off his hat to mop sweat from his bald dome. "Hell, gents, I'm with yuh. But when I was up there before, this Valentine Ross showed me a lease all legal from the State to cut timber. I got to obey the law."

"Yuh call this law?" Ward demanded angrily, and half rose up; blood suffused his face, as he fell back with a groan.

Yager took up the cudgel for his old pal. "Yeah, Godey. They near murdered Sam and they've killed plenty of our men. Is that law? Is it law to cut off our water supply and steal our stock?"

"You gents went off half-cocked when yuh attacked them lumberjacks," replied the sheriff stoutly. "They had a right to defend

95

themselves. And Ross claims Vasco Torquila's the one who took yore cows."

"You're a fool," cried Yager. "Ross pulled the wool over your eyes, Godey. If you feel so, get out of here, we don't want your help. As for me I stand for Ward and Maravilla." He stuck out his square jaw, glaring at the sheriff.

Fighting talk was hot; the air was tense with the aroused passions of the ranchers. These men were leaders of the Maravilla country through the great area drained by the river; rough, self-made men, used to the saddle and gun, to protecting themselves. There were plenty more of them in Bowie and through the land.

The black shadow of wholesale death hung over the once lovely range.

"Jest a sec, gents," a voice broke in, and surprised eyes turned on the tall Ranger.

As he spoke, easily, with the born power of a great leader, they listened under the spell of that soft but commanding voice:

"Gents, the Southwest Lumber Company ain't so easy to beat. I callate they've switched off yore water to madden yuh. Why else? They know as well as you do they can't run them logs through with yore vigilantes gunnin' 'em with rifles from long range; they can't quit work ev'ry few minutes to chase yore men. Ross is too smart to draw yuh all up there 'less he's ready and wishin' for it. And if he's ready it means yuh run into hell agin."

The sharpness of his logic could not be denied. It gave the hot-headed ranchers pause.

"What would yuh suggest, then, Harris?" Ward asked.

"I've had some experience organizin'," the Ranger told them carefully. "Now, people can get along on what water there is for a few days till we find what Ross is up to."

"And how, mister," asked Mayor Yager, "are we to do that?"

"I'll guarantee to let yuh know. In the meantime arm yore men but do it quiet-like."

He nodded shortly, swung and strolled out; he had made his point and to speak further would not help. Hatfield walked back to Morton's room and looked in on the bronc buster.

"Feeling better?" the Ranger asked.

Morton nodded, grinned. "Sorta like a hunka chewed leather, but I'll be okay after a rest."

The conference in Ward's room broke up, and the men came out, sifting around the big house. Sheriff Godey was first to leave;

he went out and through Morton's window Hatfield saw him throwing a stiff leg over his saddle.

"Reck'n I'll be ridin'," the Ranger told Ban, "but I'll be back. Keep yore eye peeled."

As he stepped quickly out into the big living room, Shorty, the squat waddy, eyes gleaming red, ran in from the front and pulled up suddenly. He pointed an accusing finger at Jim Hatfield.

"Gents!" he bellowed. "That there hombre's the one who snatched that scarface lumberman from us! I reckernized his voice."

Shorty was going for his gun; John Ogalvie, and Mayor Yager, too, were swearing as they dropped hands to their holstered Colts. The ranchers froze, however; for with his back to the side wall, Hatfield had his blue-steel six-shooter out and up, hammer spur back under his thumb. The menacing black eye that was the muzzle seemed to cover every heart in the room and they stopped as they were.

Furious eyes, accusing the tall jigger, burned in their heads. The sheriff, called by the cowboys outside, came rushing back, threw himself off his horse and came up on the porch.

"Boys," drawled Hatfield, "yuh've got a name for goin' off half-cocked and yuh're doin' it agin. I've told yuh I'm with yuh, and if yuh don't b'lieve me I'll jest hafta prove it. Now I'm leavin' but yuh'll hear from me again."

"He's a spy," cried Senator Ardmore, "a spy for the lumbermen!"

"Put up that gun," Godey called from the front.

Hatfield took a step back, into Ban Morton's room. The bronc buster had heard the talk outside, and he was watching his big friend, the man who had saved him, with troubled eyes. His gunbelt, with six-guns in it, hung from the back of a chair but he had made no move to shoot the Ranger in the back or cover him.

"Jim — Jim! It ain't true, is it?" he gasped.

The gray-green eyes were dark; Jim Hatfield knew that this event had set him back in his job; he must regain the confidence of Maravilla, even as he worked against the unseen enemies who raged for his life.

"Yuh'll see me agin, Morton," he growled. "Keep yore eye peeled while I'm gone."

Jim Hatfield was at the wide open window, and in a moment he was outside it. A shrill whistle brought Goldy and the Ranger mounted from the window sill, as a rush of men started through Morton's room. A bullet spanged the air, nipping at his Stetson; then he heard Morton's voice. "Cut it out," he bellowed. "Hold it. Yuh've got him all wrong, gents!"

The Ranger did not wish to fire upon the ranchers; though misguided they were decent men whom he meant to aid. He swung at full speed around the line of barns, as armed waddies started for him from the front.

Goldy opened up, legs flashing at full speed that drew swiftly away from the mounted cowboys, whooping it up and shooting after Hatfield. There was plenty of cover to the southeast, and the Ranger headed for it, doubling around to lose them in a burst of clever backtracking.

A mile from the Bar W he rode from the mesquite onto the rutted dirt road leading into Bowie.

"How'd that Shorty waddy reckernize my voice," he mused. "He didn't know me from Buffalo Bill when he fust come in."

He swung, to look back from a little knoll, at the big spread of the ranch, the rolling, beautiful land where the stock grazed so peacefully. The sun was red as a ruby over the hills where lurked the deadly minions of the Southwest Company.

A rider was heading along the road, toward him; he caught the sudden shine on the star pinned to the hombre's vest. That was Sheriff Godey and Hatfield wished to contact him. He drew back, waited until the officer was abreast of him, then shoved Goldy out on the road.

Godey's bearded lips opened in a gasp; his hand twitched toward his gun, as he took in the great fighting man, the thin, quick hands, Colts ready in black oiled holsters. His brows drew into a worried line, for he realized the big man had him.

"I'll ride with yuh, Sheriff," drawled Hatfield, "and I'll guarantee yuh'll be interested. Yuh got nuthin' to fear from me."

Godey cursed, but he was relieved. The two swung toward Bowie, Godey still wary, wondering what it was all about. Something that sounded like a giant fly buzzed between them, to spang into the bushes fringing the Maravilla's bed.

"That was a bullet," Godey gasped.

"Rifle and a mile off," the Ranger said. "It'd take a lucky shot to hit us."

Godey gave him a sharp look. Then he saw the silver star, set on a silver circle, emblem of the Texas Rangers, cupped in Hatfield's palm. "Jumpin' Jee," the Sheriff cried. "So that's it! What's yore handle,

101

Ranger?"

"Jim Hatfield. McDowell sent me."

"Great. I've heard tell of yuh. But yuh ain't alone?"

Hatfield shrugged. "For a while. But there's four hunderd fightin' waddies in Maravilla."

Godey mopped his face. "Yeah, but Ward won't trust yuh now, after what that Shorty claims. It ain't true, is it?"

Hatfield told him about it. "It was a smart play," Godey agreed, "if it hadn't backfired, Ranger. Yuh shore bit off somethin' when yuh come to help these ranchers. I don't know which side of the fence to drop on."

"The Southwest Lumber Company," Hatfield told him, "has busted ev'ry law Texas ever made and is huntin' more."

Godey gave an explosive sigh. "Glad to hear it. I'll fight shoulder to shoulder with Ward. On'y — that timber lease worries me. Them hills're the State's, to use as Austin says. These cowmen run stock on open range."

"McDowell'll look up that lease. I want yuh to send a man yuh kin trust up to the telegraph office with a wire. I'll write what I want done and yuh make sure there's no slip. Yuh any idee who held up the complaints?"

Godey shook his head. "Mebbe it was done at the Austin end," he suggested.

"Mebbe. I'll find out."

Darkness had fallen before they reached Bowie. Lights twinkled in homes, saloons were briskly shining; horses and teams stood at hitch-racks, and around a tree-shaded plaza in the center. Yells of drinking waddies rang on the night air as the Ranger and Godey dismounted in the shadows near the west end of the plaza.

"Ever hear tell of an hombre here called Fat Phil?" Hatfield inquired.

"Why, shore. That must be the gambler who sits in Jack's back rooms. He's fat as a hogshead. Why?"

Hatfield informed him about Scarface's report to Ross. Godey slapped his leg. "That's right. I seen that Scarface one night with Phil!"

The Ranger, by the light of a match Godey held for him, wrote out a note, resting the paper on his saddle. "Askin' Mc-Dowell to check the Southwest's sales up to now, and that lease," he explained. "Get it off quick as yuh can and have yore man fetch the reply to Bowie. We'll split; I got an idee, and I don't want to be seen yet with yuh."

"I savvy." Godey took the penciled message and rode off.

The tall man led Goldy to the shadows cast by a great live-oak growing near the edge of the plaza, left his pet, and crossed to the awninged sidewalk. Yager's, the big store, was open, as were the saloons; there were armed cowboys around. Jack's place was next door to the store and the Ranger entered, stood at the end of the bar. A barkeeper came to serve him, and he ordered whiskey.

"Is Fat Phil here?" Hatfield asked in a low voice when it was shoved out.

"In the back room, dealin' faro."

One by one, Jim Hatfield was swiftly marking down the enemies of Maravilla, of Texas. He sensed, from what he had come upon, gigantic menace to the state; there was more to it than Maravilla, and he must check it before it grew too large to stop. That map, now, that cut a swathe through the central and southern parts of Texas —

He was threading a way through the crowd to the rear. A closed door confronted him and he knocked.

"Come in," a thick, heavy voice ordered.

Hatfield opened the door, stepped through. A dozen gamblers sat at a long table. The dealer was an enormously fat man, bulging over his chair; he had flabby jowls, a round body and a round head; he was extremely gross, and the expression on his face was that of a pig. He looked up, all his motions very slow, and frowned at the Ranger.

"Want to sit in?" he growled.

The Ranger shook his head. "Like a word with yuh."

Fat Phil got up; it took him seconds to accomplish it. He had on a gunbelt, shoved out taut by his enormous paunch. His foxy little eyes, set pudgily in the folds of fat, gleamed, and he waddled to a side door after waving a hand to his assistant to take the game over.

Out in the dark side alley, Fat Phil asked softly, "Yes? Who's that?"

The Ranger didn't forget. "S. — W. — L." he replied.

Fat Phil grunted. "Follow me. You're early." He swung around back of Jack's. Close at hand was a small, dark shack which Fat Phil entered. His gruff voice reached Hatfield: "Come in. You can wait here."

Alert, not sure that the password used in the hills was the one for Bowie, not at all certain Fat Phil was not leading him into a trap, the tall jigger stepped inside the inky hut.

Chapter VII
Raid

A chair scraped. "Sit down and make yourself comfortable," ordered Fat Phil. "The boss'll be busy a while but then he'll be along. Have a drink." Fat Phil shut the door, drew the window curtain; he struck a match and touched the guttering yellow flame to a candle standing on the board table. The light shone on his wicked face, glinted from a bottle and glasses.

"So you're a minin' expert," growled Phil. "I guess Ross showed you that coal seam, and told you where to come."

"Shore." Hatfield let Phil call the turns.

"We need a man like you, and you'll come in handy the next few days, a new face, till we're set. D'you know if they finished off that nosey Morton?"

"Purty near; but he was saved."

Fat Phil swore. "He won't be long. The chief hates his guts. We got to be rid of men like Morton and Ward; well, Friday'll do it, we'll settle their hash then. I wouldn't be surprised if the chief had our man at the Bar W kill Morton tonight, though; he's got a real grudge against that bronc buster. I suppose Ross told you what went on here?"

Hatfield had to be careful; he couldn't show too much ignorance nor yet too much knowledge. He hoped to draw further valuable information from Fat Phil, who had evidently been told to watch for a mining expert.

"And how much," the Ranger asked, tentatively, "is there in it for me, Phil?"

"Why, a fortune! There's five in the main Syndicate, but we'll cut you in the way we did Ross if you're valuable enough. Once you get out that coal, there's an iron deposit up in Pecos, and do you know much about oil?"

The Ranger nodded as he drank. "It costs real money to get such stuff out, Phil; we'll need a railroad spur for that coal."

"Don't worry. Once we win here we'll be rich enough to float the whole shebang."

"Labor, that's the most expensive —"

"Not with us, pal. Torquila's the answer. We'll own the entire state of Texas."

Yells, gunshots, sounded outside. Hatfield growled, "What's that?"

Fat Phil chuckled. "All accordin' to plan.

Keep sittin'."

There was the pounding of many hoofs and the whoops of cowboys; then the hubbub died off in the east distance and quiet settled over Bowietown.

The Ranger resumed his careful probing. He was, actually, a mining expert; now he was digging for nuggets, digging the gross hombre who squatted across the table like a loathsome crab. He put admiration into his next remark.

"Torquila — there's a great feller."

Fat Phil was laughing, belly silently shaking. "Yeah, Torquila's a great one! That's the best trick of all!"

"Yeah? How so?"

But Fat Phil only replied cryptically, "If everybody knew that, hell would break loose. You'll find out, when you're a member of the Syndicate. No one else knows, up here. The chief's the craftiest devil you ever heard of. Take my advice and make good on the first job he gives you; he may have you kill Morton, since they missed him today."

"I understand this Morton's caused plenty trouble."

"True, but that's not the real reason. We need the Bar W. Maybe you can get Morton the way it was done with Sam Ward."

"How'd they manage it?"

"Oh, Ward was a nuisance; that corridor, you see" — Fat Phil enjoying his superior show of knowledge to this new and supposedly trustworthy thief, broke off, put a fat finger warningly to his lips.

Horses, ridden up, were just outside. A heavy knock on the door, and Fat Phil's pudgy hand went to his gun.

"Yes? Who's that?" growled Fat Phil.

"S. — W. — L.," a harsh voice replied.

As Fat Phil opened and pulled back the slab door, Hatfield rose and stood against the wall. He knew that voice. In the opening stood two men, one a wide, squat figure; it was Bigjaw Haley and the muleskinner's right wrist was bandaged where the Ranger had put that slug.

"We've come in to pick up the stuff," growled Haley. "I rode on ahead with this minin' feller Ross sent —" His eyes suddenly fixed on the figure of the Ranger, off to the right behind Fat Phil.

Fat Phil, with a gasp, suspicion flaming red in his pudgy face, whirled with surprising speed. "Why, he — That —" he yelled.

"Texas Ranger!" Bigjaw Haley howled, and dug for a gun with his left hand.

Fat Phil had his weapon out, rising. The Ranger's Colt blasted straight into the fat hombre and the mountain of flesh quivered, shook violently, as the great arm dropped limp. Fat Phil hit the table, overturned it, the candle going out. The so-called mining expert, behind Haley, let out a yell and turned to bolt into the night. In the sudden dark, the candle smoking on the floor, "Drop yore gun, Haley," Hatfield warned. "This is the next time!"

But Haley was rattled; panic surged through him at sound of that crisp, cold voice, the voice of the hombre who was the only one who had ever made him feel fear. The pistol in Haley's hand blared, as his fingers tightened spasmodically; Hatfield felt the wind of the bullet close to his face.

The Ranger's Colt spat blue-yellow flame; the broad muleskinner's arms flew out, his weapon clanked against the log wall, thudded dully in the dirt. Haley fell in the doorway, a bullet straight through his evil brain.

Acrid powder smoke drifted to the flared nostrils of the Ranger as he rapidly pushed fresh shells into his warm pistol. His ears sang with the boom of the heavy guns in the confined shack.

No one came running at sound of the shots. But a great chorus of yells, and the rapid beat of hundreds of hoofs, took Jim Hatfield outside; he stepped across the dead

110

muleskinner and went through the dark alley toward Main Street. He turned into Jack's, and the saloon was deserted save for the bartenders.

"Where's everybody?" asked the Ranger.

"Vasco Torquila jest raided the Circle Five," a barkeep said. "Killed a couple waddies and run off a bunch of cows. Set fire to some barns, and the boys're on his trail."

"Leavin' the town wide open for Ross," decided Hatfield.

He stepped to the front window, looked out. A large band of mounted men came pushing in from the west. At their head rode Valentine Ross, the pasty-faced devil, top boss of the Southwest Lumber Company. Arrogant, sneering, Ross looked from side to side for enemies as he entered the capital of his foes, the ranchers. With him were two hundred armed muleskinners and lumberjacks, in corduroys, carrying Winchester rifles ready for instant use, pistols strapped to burly waists, a fierce looking, warlike army.

They stopped at Yager's, the big general store, still open. Ross got down and a bunch of his men crowded up on the porch behind him; others commanded the plaza and street.

Hatfield went back to the side door, slid

111

out and went to Tincan Alley, behind the buildings. From a rear window he looked into the big store, filled with boxes of supplies of all kinds. A main counter ran from front to rear; there were smaller counters, one for dry goods, another for hardware.

Ross and his 'jacks were already in.

The boss stood up front, and facing him from behind the long counter, an open window at his back, stood Mayor Smiley Yager, glaring in rage as Ross coldly uttered his commands, the rasping voice penetrating to where Hatfield watched, at the back.

"Good evenin', Mayor Yager," Ross said sardonically. "We've come to do a little business with you, seein' we're such good neighbors. Want whiskey and your best tobacco; and we could use some of those canned goods boxed over there."

Under menacing guns, Yager and his three clerks had to stand. John Ogalvie was in there, too, and so was Keith of the Running R. Evidently they had just ridden back from the Bar W, and not yet started for the Circle 5, burning after Torquila's attack. They were trapped inside the store by Ross and his killers.

Yager spluttered in fury as he cursed Ross. "Damn your heart and soul! Get out of my store. Get out! I wouldn't sell you 'jacks anything but rat poison."

Ross frowned. "You'll sell us what we want, seein' as how you've cut off our supplies from the railroad, Yager. Tote that stuff out, boys."

Ready hands began carrying out the boxes of canned goods, bottles of liquor and bundles of tobacco.

Ranger Hatfield watched for a clear bead on Valentine Ross. He had put Fat Phil out of the criminal Syndicate threatening Texas; he hoped to diminish the Syndicate again. But the thin hombre was covered by the counters and by the moving bodies of his men, thick inside the store.

Mayor Yager suddenly gave a howl of fury; he snatched his gun out, fired a hasty shot that whirled close over Ross's narrow head. The mayor dived backward out of the window, as Ross fired back.

Ogalvie and George Keith both went for their Colts, but rifles and revolvers poured a death hail into them. Ogalvie went down, mortally wounded, life-blood gushing from a dozen wounds; Keith's right arm was shattered and he stood, proudly waiting for death.

"Let him have it," bawled Ross, gulping with fury.

Hatfield opened fire through his window.

His spaced, accurate slugs knocked over one 'jack after another, stung the mob to insane fury. They placed him after the first couple of explosions, and a concerted rush was made toward the window, as they covered it with a thick hail of death.

Ross was down behind the counter. "Get him," he shrieked.

Armed men from outside started around the big store, coming through the alleys. The crashing guns, the yells of hate, made up a horrid bedlam.

There was no cover at hand. The Ranger ducked past the alleyway, heard singing lead as they glimpsed his moving figure. He ran toward the road, past the saloon; they were in full hue and cry on his trail. He paused under the awning a moment; and Sheriff Godey galloped across the Plaza, yelling, guns in hand.

"Get back, Godey," bawled Hatfield. But in the din the sheriff failed to hear the warning; he rode his horse straight up to the store, into the massed gunmen, never faltering in his mad courage, the courage of an old-time law officer.

Hatfield tried to distract them by fanning slugs into the 'jacks; but it was impossible to save Godey, and bullets poured into the sheriff. He fell from his horse and was cut up under the dancing hoofs of the many horses and mules, terrified by the shooting.

Ross came out on the store porch, and saw Hatfield. "That's the man we want," he howled.

A bullet smacked into the wall an inch from the Ranger. Two hundred guns were turning upon him. They were coming at him, roaring on his trail. Goldy stood under a tree, across the road, and Hatfield, Colts barking, melted among the shadows.

From the side of the store, a gun flashed, again and again, and among the wildly fired volley, it seemed to search out the Ranger. He felt the bite of a bullet along his ribs, that stung with horrible agony; he set his teeth, ran to the golden sorrel. There was, in his eyes, the dark coldness of an Arctic storm.

He must, he knew, hurry back to the Bar W; even now it might be too late to save Morton. From the defunct Fat Phil he had obtained information that had made it possible for him to envisage the ruthless, far-reaching plans of the Syndicate. The significance of the map dotted with letters, that he had seen in Ross's shack in the hills smote him, spelling disaster to the vast state of Texas.

As the Ranger rode hell-for-leather westward, a man stamped with an insane fury inside Phil's cabin where Bigjaw Haley and the fat man lay in stiff, ghastly death.

"Damn him!" he raved, "damn him! I'll pay any man five thousand dollars for that Ranger's hide!"

A tall, bony hombre, slouched in the doorway, hissed in sympathetic rage. The glow of his eyes in the dimness was phosphorescent as a cat's.

"You were right, Chief," he snarled. "He's a Texas Ranger. Made us more trouble than the county law and cowmen combined."

"I'll get him," the chief promised, voice thick with his anger. "I'll kill him myself!"

Through the alley between Haley's store and Jack's Saloon could be seen the hundreds of pack animals, forming into a long train under the whips of the cursing, shouting muleskinners. The caravan, dust rising under beating hoofs, was started west for the hills. Square wooden boxes showed, balanced on either flank of the pack animals. An army of guards, with rifles and pistols, rode the flanks and brought up the rear.

"Shall I set everything as you ordered for Friday?" inquired the green-eyed man.

"Certainly. Next Friday."

"How about Ward — and Morton?"

"They'll be dead inside an hour; I saw to

that, when I found how things had gone. I'll smash these cowmen into the ground. Can't let a few stubborn old fools ruin my plans."

"See you Friday, then?"

"Okay. And make sure there's no slip."

"There won't be, Chief. Listen, that so-called minin' expert came runnin' out with a face like a ghost, said he quit before he started. He didn't like the way that Ranger acted. I took care of him; so we'll have to find another man."

The Chief's teeth ground together. "The Ranger again," he snarled. "I'll eat his heart when I catch him."

Chapter VIII
The Blow of Torquila

Ban Morton awoke, a cold sweat on his lank body. He had nerves attuned to his wild, outdoor life, almost animal in sensitivity; besides, his injuries ached, muscles stiff from the terrible beating he had taken from Bigjaw Haley, though with the steel flexibility of youth he was fast regaining his strength.

The silver moon streamed in the open window of his little bedroom. Across the wide living room of the great ranch house, through a door crack, he could see a streak of yellow that came from Sam Ward's chamber.

"Guess Elsie's up tendin' him," he muttered.

He tried to sleep again but a second time started awake, that cold sweat all over him.

Ban lay, intently listening. Horrid terror, a black pall of death, lay heavy upon the Maravilla country. It seethed with danger, men

118

were not safe in their homes. A gigantic, evil brain planned destruction for them. But there should be armed, alert guards around the ranch; those were strict orders.

Morton knew he was in constant jeopardy; a hidden enemy pined for his death; someone had tried to drygulch him and that trap had been set especially for him in the hills, when they had drawn him up through his love for Black Rascal.

And, as he stared at the lighter rectangle of the window he saw the tip of a peaked sombrero stealthily rising.

Silently he reached out a hand, gripped the cool butt of his .45 gun, hanging from the chair in its leather holster belt.

A faint scraping from the window, then the sheen of light on a long metal barrel; Ban threw himself out of his cot, streamers of pain shooting through his aching limbs as he hit the boards of the floor. He was blinded by the flash of the rifle in the window; the bed hopped as the long bullet ripped through the blanket, mattress and spring on which he had been lying, and splintered the floor a few inches from his elbow as it buried itself in the pine flooring.

Ban Morton let go rapidly, three shots, through the open window. The rifle clanged on the sill, and as the gun flashes that had blinded his eyes ceased, he saw that the opening was vacant. Ears ringing with the pent-up explosions, he heard running steps, the guttural cursing of a wounded man.

"Reck'n I singed him," he growled, and, coming up on his knee, scurried to the window and cautiously stuck out his head. He saw a dark, stooped figure duck around the rear of the house, out of his sight.

"Hey, boys," he sang out, to call the sentries supposed to be guarding the Bar W and Sam Ward.

No one answered him; even the bunkhouse, where day and relief shifts should be sleeping, failed to come to life.

The moon lit the dome of the mighty sky, dotted with star points; the soft west wind rustled the oaks and alders and the mesquite, bringing with it the scent of aromatic blossoms. In the distance a horse whinnied — Black Rascal had heard his master's call.

Ban Morton swore, wondering where everybody was. He strapped on his gunbelt, and, worried about Elsie and her father, went through his door, stepped into the living room. It was late and the fire in the big fireplace had burned down to an ash-encrusted mass of ruby coals.

There was still a light in Ward's room, and he heard Old Sam coughing; then a sharp sound which he knew was Ward banging the floor with a stick, calling his daughter.

"Elsie!" Ban said, but the girl didn't answer.

Morton went over and entered the rancher's chamber. Ward lay in bed, dry lips working.

"Ban, what were them shots? I been callin' Elsie a long while, my water tipped over and I'm dry as alkali. Callate the pore kid's wore out, nursin' me; I thought I heard her voice a while back but she didn't come."

A single candle burned golden in its stick, on a small table close to the bed. Morton slid around and picked up Ward's tin mug and pitcher, lying in a wet spot on the floor.

"I'll get yuh a drink, be back in a jiffy," he told the wounded man cheerfully, and, not to alarm him, he added, "Guess the night guard seen some spooks outside and let their Colts go."

Death was closing in upon young Ban, on Old Sam; forces too powerful for them to defeat plotted to destroy them.

Ban could not guess this; he felt only a vague uneasiness, as he took the jug and passed through the living room, headed for the well outside; he thought he'd draw fresh water, cool and invigorating, for Ward. He came to Elsie's room on his way along the

121

hall. Her door was open and a candle gut-
tered on the dressing table. Her bed was
empty, though it was turned down, as
though she had got up after retiring.

Deep lines corrugated the bronc buster's
forehead. "Huh," he grunted. "Mebbe she's
in the kitchen." But she wasn't nor was she
outside. She did not answer his soft calls.

He stepped into the shadowy yard, unable
to shake off that icy dread that gripped him.
Then he saw the circle of horsemen, silently
sitting their saddles. They sighted him and
their guns rose, cries in Spanish challenging
him. The voices, the sheen of the moonlight
on the crossed bandilleros heavy with
cartridges, the peaked hats, warned him
who they were.

"Mexes!" he gasped.

He leaped back, as, when he failed to reply
to them, they opened fire. He ran through
the hall, and as he reached the entry into
the living room he saw a big Mexican crossing the front toward Ward's room, behind
him half a dozen renegades, cigarettes curl-
ing smoke from their brownish lips.

The leader was a giant; he wore velvet
trousers trimmed with silver conchas,
tucked into spurred boots, scarlet waistband
pulling in his paunch, a short, sleeveless
brown jacket trimmed with gold braid, and

a peaked sombrero ornamented with rows of pearl.

"Torquila!" shouted Morton. He had never seen the Mexican bandit chief but had heard him described.

The huge bandit was framed against the dying fire. Ban Morton saw the dark, cruel face, blotches of mustache and goatee, the white teeth between sneering lips. At sound of Morton's cry Torquila whirled, gun in hand.

"Cien nil diablos!" he shouted harshly.

For an instant he failed to place the bronc buster. That instant was fatal, for as his gun blasted, the slug missed Morton by a yard and Ban threw up his Colt and let go, the dropped pitcher clanging on the floor.

Torquila bellowed with anguish; he was half whirled around by the impact of the heavy bullet, and he sank, slowly, to the mat, out of Ban's sight behind the sofa and table before the fireplace.

His bandits jumped into action. A volley of bullets whirled at Morton, who threw himself flat, back of a big sideboard. The lead rapped into the walls and tore off great splinters from the sideboard.

More of Torquila's hombres crowded inside, and ran to their chief. Others cursed shrilly as they tried to kill Ban Morton.

Behind the cover of blazing guns, the Mexicans quickly carried their leader outside.

The fall of Torquila threw the bandits into confusion, and they did not stand against Morton's gunfire but scuttled out onto the veranda. He could hear their excited chatter, and, seizing his opportunity, he jumped up and ran full-tilt to Ward's room.

The rancher chieftain's eyes were wide with excitement at the mad shooting. "Where's Elsie?" he cried.

Ban Morton shook his head. He swept the candle from the table, plunging them in darkness, as he heard sounds at the windows. There was a mahogany bureau against the wall and the bronc buster dragged it up so it stood between Ward's bed and the windows.

Bullets already were coming in, Spanish curses rising outside. Ban Morton fired back, on his knees back of the bureau, protecting Ward as best he could.

"Gimme a gun!" gasped Sam. "It's hangin' on the head of my bed." In extreme pain, the old rancher showed his cool mettle, the strain of the fighting man's blood.

Ban quickly passed him his loaded Colt Frontier Model .45. Ward couldn't rise but was able to shoot from a reclining position and he helped keep the windows clean of the enemy. The heavy boom of the guns deafened them; they were fighting for their lives against overwhelming odds.

"Where in Gawd's name is Elsie?"

That was what was torturing Morton, the strange disappearance of the girl he loved. But he had to protect Ward, stay alive himself; she wasn't in the house or in hearing or she'd have come. He heard yelps of pain, knew he had made some hits.

"Burn them out — burn the gringos!" shrieked a bandit lieutenant.

In the feverish nightmare gripping Ban Morton there seemed no help, no relief. The minutes dragged like hours of torture, the insane crashes of deadly guns, the shrill yelps of the killers; and, worst of all, the stifling smell of burning hay and wood, lighted and thrown through the shattered windows. Sam was coughing, now too weak to hold his gun; he lay there with his head on the pillow. The acrid smoke bit at Morton's eyes, and anguish of uncertainty as to Elsie's fate tore his heart as though someone had stuck a knife into him.

It was only a question of minutes till the last charge of hate would bring them in upon the two pressed men, to die under the Mexicans' knives. Morton knew that; and as he groped in the smoky dark for cartridges with which to fill his hot gun, he realized it was upon them, for he was out of ammunition. He picked the last five from Ward's belt and shoved them into the cylinders of his revolver, forced to hold up his fire to conserve them.

His one slim chance to escape was to run, elude Torquila's band by speed of foot, grab a horse, that he could not take for it meant deserting Ward to die at the killers' hands.

They were inside the house, too, at the door, leaping out for a moment to fire in on the two, through the smoke. When he failed to answer, a shout of victory went up.

"We have them — now!"

They were rushing Morton, small, savage-faced bandits crowding through the door. He put up his gun, the acrid smoke twitching his eyes, sending smarting tears down his grimed cheeks, and fired twice into the bunch. But it was only a brief respite; their volley tore back at him, and he felt the ripping of a bullet through his left arm.

In such hellish confusion it was almost impossible for Ban Morton to distinguish individual sounds. Yet, as he rose up, to die in front of Sam Ward in his last stand, the brutal shouting of the Mexicans did change in character. Shots farther off boomed in the sudden strange lull.

His ears shrieked with the deafening explosions but he could hear, and his thumping heart leaped.

"Bar W — this way!" he bawled.

Yet no answering cowboy whoops came to him, and the bandits in the living room started a final charge; he emptied his Colt and cursed at them.

Shrieked orders in Spanish, the thud of many hoofs, the running beat of feet, confused Ban Morton, waiting there with Sam Ward for death.

CHAPTER IX
THE DEATH TRAIL

Within earshot of the Bar W, speeding along the ribbon of dirt road westward, Ranger Jim Hatfield heard ahead the crashing gunfire.

He had shaken off the pursuit outside of Bowie. The ardor of Ross's killers who managed to trail him for a time, cooled considerably when he shot two of them out of their saddles; the power of the golden sorrel, a fit mount for the mighty Lone Wolf, discouraged them too. After a mile they had swung back to the safety of the mob.

The widespread trouble in Maravilla, he had already diagnosed as the beginning of a greater ruin, the raiding of Texas. He intended to break the criminal Syndicate.

"Fat Phil makes one," he mused. "There bein' four left. Ross is another; Torquila third; there's two more." And one, he knew, was the chief, hidden to him but on whose trail he was riding with the keenness of a bloodhound.

"Hafta head for Torquila's hangout," he decided. Fat Phil had proved valuable, during his brief contact with the Ranger; there was a puzzle about Torquila that amused Fat Phil, and that, Hatfield sensed, might be the answer to the problem he must solve.

The wind blew in his rugged, set face as he whirled off from the river, and saw the dark shapes of the Bar W buildings. The glow of a small fire on the north side of the house framed for him the crowding figures of Mexicans, shaggy mustangs near at hand, who were pouring lead into Ward's room.

Their savage yells, and the drift of smoke to his flared nostrils, told him what was happening. And as he threw up both Colts to attack, he hoped he was not too late. He needed Ward and he wanted to save the stalwart old rancher from death. Such a man as Ward deserved help.

He touched the great sorrel, galloping in with flashing piston legs, with a spur; Goldy whirled and they came in from the northwest, the terrific Colts of the Ranger blasting into the bunched bandidos. The efficiency of his fire as he poured bullets into the nucleus of the attackers, picked with his unerring accuracy and coolness in battle, quickly threw confusion into their ranks.

A shrill screeching rose. "The Ranger! The Ranger!" For some of these men had tried to take him, up there at the lumber camp.

As he hit the end of his run, the sorrel spun on a dime, zigzagging back through the wild slugs the bandits returned. But already they were mounting and riding off hell-for-leather southward into the darkness.

Smashing them, he turned and came back, ever closer to the house, one wall of which was afire. He saw the bunch that had been inside, running and leaping off the porch, hitting their saddles in the panic of retreat.

With the horde on its way, sending bullets back at him, he pushed to the north side where the bandits had dragged an old wagon into which they had thrown several bales of dry hay; this burned fiercely, flames licking at the wooden house, smoke pouring through the windows, sucked by the indraft. The Ranger hit the dirt and grabbed the wagon pole. He dragged the cart off and with his poncho, unfurled from Goldy's saddle, he beat out the burning boards.

From the north, in the distance, he heard shrill cowboy whoops. The Ranger vaulted the side rail of the long porch and hurried into the house.

"Ward! Morton!" he shouted.

There was no reply for a moment; he

stood there, faint light rays on his rugged features, powerful figure in a listening attitude, smoke acrid in his flared nostrils. He started toward Ward's room, muscles rippling with the flowing grace of a panther. Cold fury was upon him, for he thought Ward and Morton must have died.

"Now where the hell's that night guard?" he muttered.

His boot skidded under him; he looked down, saw a dark pool of blood. "Ward," he called again, at the splintered door.

"Hey. Who's that?" Morton's voice, husky with fresh hope, answered him.

"It's Jim, Ban. The Mexes've gone. Light up. Where's all yore waddies?"

Cursing in relief, Morton struck a match, found the candle and lit it. His face was grimed with sweat and powder smoke. Anxiously he looked at Ward, and the tall Ranger, spurs jingling, crossed and bent over the old rancher.

"Still kickin'," Hatfield drawled. "He's fainted."

Ban pumped his hand. "Yuh saved us! We were at the last gasp, Jim. I knowed they was crazy when they said yuh was a spy."

"Hafta see 'bout that," Hatfield told him. "What happened to yore guards?"

"Dunno. And — Elsie's gone." Rapidly,

the distressed Morton described the events of the night, the attempt to shoot him through his window, the strange disappearance of Elsie, the terrible fight with the bandits.

Hatfield swung on his spurs and Ban limped out after him; paused to light the living-room lamp. Hatfield stopped under Morton's window, stooped to pick up a black circle lying there. Ban held a match for the Ranger, and saw it was a peaked sombrero.

"One of them Mexes tried to drygulch me!" he cried.

Hatfield grunted. He carried the peaked hat, trimmed with tiny silver horseshoes, into the house, looked it over carefully in the lamplight. There was blood on the sweatband, under the bullet hole.

"Yuh clipped him, Ban," Hatfield drawled.

Between his long fingers he picked out several strands of brownish hair stuck to the blood.

From Ban's account, Torquila was wounded; that was a help, thought the officer. The bronc buster controlled himself by a great effort; an overpowering dread clutched at Ban's vitals and Hatfield understood how much he loved Elsie.

"Get some whiskey and we'll see to Ward,"

ordered Hatfield. They went and poured a drink between Sam's clenched teeth.

"Elsie — Elsie honey," the old rancher moaned as consciousness returned. "They took her out with no trouble," the rancher mused. "Must've been somebody she knowed or she'd've called out and Morton would've heard, me too."

It only clinched what he had already deduced.

The yells of approaching cowboys sounded closer. Ward looked up at them. "It's okay, Boss," Morton told him, taking a cloth to wipe sweat from the big man's tortured face. "Jim's here and he beat 'em off."

Ward stared at the tall fellow. "Say — they claimed yuh was a spy! Shorty and all —"

"That's a lie," cried Ban. "He's shore proved he's with us, Boss."

"Well, reckon yuh're right, Ban," Ward whispered.

Heavy steps banged on the porch, more shouts. "That's the men come back," growled Morton. Teeth gritted, he turned and went out. Hatfield slouched in the doorway, watching.

A bunch of waddies, headed by Foreman Nevada Lewis, crowded inside.

"Yuh was ordered not to leave the yard,"

Morton snapped. "While yuh was chasin' through the night, Torquila's gang hit us, near kilt the Boss and kidnaped Miss Elsie. What's the idee?" Ban Morton was furious.

"Say, who's askin' all them questions?" Nevada Lewis snarled. "I'm s'posed to be foreman here. I ordered the men out for a damn good reason. A bunch of rustlers started runnin' off that whole herd of cows we was movin' east, and we hadda stop 'em."

Morton's gaze met the saturnine eyes of Lewis, bristling up to him. "Call me a liar," howled Lewis, threateningly, "and I'll air yore hide, yuh danged, sneakin' dude." The foreman went for his gun, rage possessing him.

It was Hatfield's cold voice from the doorway that stopped him: "Put up yore hawgleg, Foreman!"

Nevada started, saw him as he turned his eyes; he dared not disobey that icy command. His gun slid back and the bunched punchers stared at the tall Lone Wolf.

"Why, it's that big hombre," Shorty bawled, "the man who snatched Scarface from us. It's the spy!"

"Hold it, yuh fools," bellowed Morton.

They held it; not so much at Ban's warning as at the Ranger's look when he came

134

out to face them. His Colts hung ready; but it was the spell of the man that kept them from trying to draw.

Before him, Hatfield thought, stood a decent bunch — most. Shorty Davis, Long John Betts, "Arizonny," all honest perspiring faces. He came to a halt half a dozen feet from Nevada Lewis, whose Stetson was pulled down to his hard eyes.

"There is a spy in the room," Hatfield said silkily. "Only it ain't me. Nevada, take off yore hat."

"Why?" snarled Lewis. His bony hands hung close to his six-guns.

"Yuh want to know and I'll tell yuh. Yuh're the spy who's been passin' inside information to Ross. But tonight yuh overstepped yoreself." He addressed the bunch, "Any of yuh men see Lewis, after he ordered yuh all out, bunkhouse and night guard?"

Come to think of it, nobody had, not until the foreman rode to meet them as they hurried home at sight of the fire.

"What yuh drivin' at?" demanded Lewis.

"Yuh led the men off, Lewis, started 'em and sneaked back, called out Elsie Ward and handed her over to the kidnapers. Borrowed a hat from a Mex, tried to kill Morton. Take off yore Stetson."

"Yuh lie! Go to hell!"

135

Shorty suddenly swept the foreman's hat off. The saturnine hombre's hair was matted with dried blood over a swelling large as a goose egg, which he had tried to hide by keeping his Stetson down.

"That's where Morton creased yuh, Lewis. I'll give you a chance pervidin' yuh tell me who —"

Nevada's eyes flamed hate. He leaped behind Shorty, gun flashing out. The Colt exploded but the boom seemed double and the foreman's slug cracked the floor between the Ranger's wide boots. Nevada, right back of Shorty, threw up his head in a convulsive, snapping movement, then folded up on the mat.

"Right between the eyes," gasped Shorty, staring down at the dead body. "Say, yuh cut it mighty close, mister. I got a haircut from yore bullet. Fust time I ever been glad I ain't no taller."

A wisp of smoke rose from the Ranger's Colt barrel as it slid back into its place. Hatfield turned and strode to Ward's room, Morton after him, the punchers bunching in the doorway.

"I'm ridin'," Hatfield told the rancher. "Whatever yuh do, don't let yore followers attack the lumbermen till yuh hear from me. It's cut-and-dried to wipe yuh out; so do as

I order and wait!"

"Where yuh headin', Jim?" Ban Morton asked.

"Hope to fetch back Elsie, for one thing."

"Lemme go too," begged Morton.

"Me, too," Shorty cried, and they all wanted to go.

"Someone's got to stick here and guard Ward," Hatfield told them. "Me'n Ban can do it." To Ward he said softly, "Now take it easy. We'll bring her back."

Outside, he drew Shorty aside. "Who told yuh I was the man snatched Scarface?"

Shorty's honest face was puzzled; he scratched his sandy head. "Why, hell — come to think, Marshal Alf Betts of Bowie slips up to me and says, 'Is it true that big jigger's the man saved Scarface? See if yuh can say.' That made me think I reckernized yore voice."

"So yuh went off half-cocked," growled Morton.

Thud of hoofs from the north sent them outside; dark shapes of burly riders swept down, and, pausing outside the light circle, a rough voice hailed, "Who's that? Vasco — Lewis?"

"The lumbermen!" bawled Shorty, and his six-gun opened fire on the invaders.

A blast of guns flared back in reply. "Take

137

cover," Hatfield yelled. Two Bar W men had been hit; one seriously. Slugs were tearing into the wood, through the night air on the soft wind.

Down behind the rail, the steps, the cowboys poured lead at the enemy. But the 'jacks did not stand; whirling, they rode full-tilt back.

"Come to see how Lewis and Torquila made out," muttered the Ranger. He knew there were a couple of hundred gunmen a few miles above; the half hundred could hold the ranch but could not defeat Ross's ferocious crew in the open. They were worn out from their long ride, the wild goose chase Lewis had sent them on.

"Let's ride, Ban," Hatfield ordered.

They headed south a few minutes later, Morton on Black Rascal, the Ranger on the golden sorrel. The two horses traveled at a pace-eating clip, under a silver moon. They crossed the Maravilla, its bed nearly dry.

"Don't yuh figger mebbe they'd take her up into the hills?" inquired Ban.

The officer glanced sideward at his young companion; Morton's mouth was a firm line.

"Callate they'll head straight for Torquila's with him wounded — and other reasons.

Pick up their trail pretty quick and check it."

The land gently sloped up from the valley. Black shapes of tortured mesquite, shadows of trees, flickering of countless fireflies, were about them; in their ears the steady clip-clop of the hoofs, and the piping of frogs and night creatures. They topped the divide in the darkness, and pushed down through the wild fastnesses of the Big Bend country.

Dawn found them sitting their horses on the north bank of the Rio Grande, wide flowing between shifting, sandy shores.

The Ranger was deep in thought. The stunning blows dealt Maravilla; the expert riposte of the arch-fiend he sought, at each move he made; the savage, efficiency spy system of the enemy, told him he must hurry, and strike unerringly at the heart of the horror if he would win. He must not fail; Texas depended on him, and death snapped at his heels.

"Hafta see Torquila," he mused, " 'sides tryin' to rescue Elsie. Marshal Betts looks harmless, but he set Shorty after me. They acted so quick yesterday, must've bin a right smart hombre present; mebbe the one I'm after."

Cactus grew thick here in the flats, of every variety from tiny hairy balls to giants thirty feet high, branching out in eerie pipe-shapes; thick barrel cactus; on the mesquite ridges, green and yellow with star-white blooms, flourished coarse chino and grama grasses. Here were the yucca and prickly pear, catclaw and bayonet, aromatic creosote with oily yellow blossoms; the low, stiff greasewood favored the alkaline soil; feathery huisache trees rustled in the morning breeze. The rippling wash of the river was a grateful sound and men and animals drank.

Red streamers rose in the eastern sky as they crossed the Rio to pick up the south trail. Alert road-runners darted from the path of the big horses, one golden, the other ebony; ladinos, tough, brush-ranging wild cows, galloped off, making a "pop" that could be heard half a mile away when they plunged into the dense tangled undergrowth.

"More blood," said Hatfield, pointing to a dark spot on the spiny, flat green leaf of a prickly pear. "Guess yuh wounded him bad, Ban."

The bronc buster was a good tracker but he was amazed at the skill of the Ranger. It was Hatfield who had certified that the bandido had brought Elsie this far. One tiny bit of white thread on a mesquite thorn had made them certain. Vasco Torquila's wound had been bleeding, kept open by the jogging of the mustang he was carried upon. A broken stick, a fresh hoof mark, drew them unerringly on.

The sun rose higher over the wilderness, and the sky became a fiery, brass oven, beating down on the Mexican land. Before them was Old Mexico.

"And Avalo," thought Hatfield.

The sun broiled them, the two grim-faced riders who pulled up their mounts and stared down at the little Mexican town.

"That's it," said Hatfield.

Adobe huts straggled in two ragged lines, along what was supposedly a road. Clothing hung in the sun; myriad naked brown children played in the shade of walls. An army of mongrel dogs, pigs, chickens and other domestic creatures roamed in and out of dooryards and houses, picking up scraps.

"Wonder what the bunch of hombres're up to?" Morton rasped, throat dry from the rising dust.

He indicated a circle of Mexicans crowded about a shallow bowl under some old trees in the plaza. Cheering came to their ears.

"Cockfightin', I reckon," Hatfield replied. "They do nothin' else down here for amusement."

"Let's go," Morton said impatiently.

"Hold it. We'll see who that is comin' in."

From the southeast a party of armed men rode into Avalo at a fast clip. The sun glinted on rifles and accoutrements. They swept up behind the buildings and, with loud shouts, surrounded the Mexicans absorbed in the spurred fighting cocks. Cries of fright rose.

"Rurales!" The armed riders pointed guns at a dozen young peons, forced them to mount spare animals.

"Torquila's bandits!" muttered Ban, hand dropping to his six-gun.

"Don't shoot."

They watched the armed band, under a lean, mustached lieutenant, turn back southeast with their captives, lost in clouds of dust. The Ranger led the way into Avalo; dogs barked at them, and sad-faced, weeping women peeked from the broken windows. The cock-fight had broken up, those who had escaped arrest hunting cover. Hatfield stopped at a dilapidated shack from which sounded loud wails.

"Senora," he called.

A fat Mexican woman, tears streaming down her cheeks, came to the door, poked fearfully out. Hatfield spoke to her in liquid, idiomatic Spanish.

"What's wrong?"

"Senor, Senor," she sobbed, "they took my son; he's only seventeen. To jail, they say. A new law against cock-fighting. What's wrong with such a sport?"

"You heard of Juan Gonzales?"

"Si, si — he was arrested so, for nothing, by the Virgin! His mother's died of a broken heart, for no word has ever come from him."

"You know Vasco Torquila?"

Her lips shut, fears streaked through her black eyes. These people lived in deadly fear of the bandit chieftain.

"I'll send yore son back to you," Hatfield promised.

She raised a brown hand, waved southeast. "That way. Five miles. A walled hacienda, like a whole town."

Hatfield tossed her a quarter, which she gratefully caught. With Morton, he saw a horse that looked fast, and they bought it, saddle and all, and hurried on.

Dusk had not yet fallen when they sighted a fortified village. Around a collection of huts, in the center of which stood a square white-washed hacienda, was a high paling topped by thorns. The gates were open, guarded by armed bandidos. A coral held hundreds of hairy Mexican ponies; there were shacks and tents. In the center was a bunch of peons, huddled together; women were about, and the Ranger estimated that Torquila's army in there must number around six hundred riders.

"Callate that's where they're holdin' Elsie. Meanwhile we'll get some sleep."

Ban Morton's face was grim with despair. How could they hope to strike such a place, swarming with murderous bandits?

CHAPTER X
JAWS OF DEATH

Hatfield touched Morton's hand to wake him from the troubled doze into which the young man had fallen.

It was entirely dark, save for the streak of moonlight penetrating the dense mesquite on the ridge. The tramp of hundreds of horses, orders in Spanish, sounded from the trail a few hundred yards south. A column of mounted bandidos, Hatfield estimated near five hundred of them, herding a couple of hundred unfortunate captives, passed close by the Ranger's hiding-place in the bush. They turned northwest.

Once they were out of earshot, Hatfield checked his Colts, mounted Goldy; Morton followed on Black Rascal. On the side opposite the gates, now barred for the night, Hatfield stopped. They sat their horses in the shadows of the high palings.

"Stay here and be ready with the spare horse; keep 'em quiet," Hatfield whispered to Ban. "I'm goin' in."

Quickly he noosed his lariat to the saddle horn; let it drop inside the enclosure. The trained sorrel stood like a statue at command, and the Ranger stood up on the saddle, grasped the top of the thorny paling. The clearing was lit by a few lanterns around the hacienda, in which showed lamps. A hundred renegades slept in the shelters or on the ground, while a few stood guard over at the gates.

Thorns tore at him as he vaulted over, knees giving when he landed, light as a leaping panther. He paused in the fence shadow a moment; the sound of a guitar strumming in the house, the high, soft voice of a young woman singing, reached his keen ears.

From patch to patch of scraggly bush he flitted. He noted the man leaning on his rifle at the front of the hacienda.

Near the back was a long window, half open and he slipped into the house.

He went swiftly, silently, toward a light shaft that half lit a long hallway to the front.

The lamplight came from a great room, furnished in rich Spanish style. On a wide, silken couch lay Vasco Torquila, the giant bandit chief. The dark, Indian face was smudged by black goatee and beard; and the flabbiness of his whole countenance gave the Ranger a start of surprise.

"Mebbe it's the wound," he mused. "Seemed to me he was a lot tougher when I glimpsed him in the hills."

A pretty Mexican senorita softly strummed the guitar, singing to soothe the injured man. Blood-soaked bandages on his right side showed where he had been hit. The music paused, as Torquila swore in fluent Spanish.

"I'll miss it, *si,*" he told the woman regretfully. "And what a sight it will be! Four hundred gringos dying in one instant. *Cara mia,* the chief's a devil but a genius too. We have as good as won, and here I die, unable to ride!" He cursed feverishly.

She stroked his brown forehead. "Never mind; you have your Rosa. Perhaps they'll change the day."

"If so, Scarface will tell my lieutenant Arturo. *Si,* nothing can stop us now; the Syndicate has won. We are wealthy beyond all dreams, Rosa. We bleed Texas to death."

"And as for the pretty American senorita?"

"She's for the chief." Torquila laughed through clenched white teeth. "It will be a good joke, Rosa. He rescues her himself, and so wins the Bar W."

Torquila closed his eyes, waved his hand; the guitar strummed again.

147

Jim Hatfield, hands swinging easily at his narrow hips, stepped into the room and looked at the giant bandit. The girl gave a gasp of alarm, small hand discording the strings. Torquila's black eyes snapped open, his bearded chin sagged at sight of the tall American.

"Madre de Dios!" gasped Torquila.

A huge brown hand started for the belts holding his pearl-handled six-shooters, hanging from the bedpost close to his head; but it paused, suspended in midair, as he stared into the steady muzzle of the Ranger's .45.

"No senor, don't shoot!" begged Rosa.

Hatfield's eyes were on Torquila, back to a blank wall so they could not steal up from behind. He did not miss his chance. "Senorita," he drawled, "get the young lady brought here today, pronto. If you give the alarm I'll kill Torquila."

She leaped up, the guitar spilling to the floor with a string-humming bang. "No," Torquila growled. "You fool, Rosa, the Chief will kill us!"

But Rosa was hurrying out, past the tall American. "I bring her," she gasped. The ominous figure of the fighting gringo awed her yet her frightened eyes were tinged with admiration, too.

"You die for this," snarled Torquila.

Steps in the hall, and Elsie Ward's voice came to him. "Rosa, where are you taking me? Please let me go home."

"Your sweetheart's here to save you."

Hatfield glided for the door. As he turned Torquila's big hand flashed to his guns, his teeth gritting in rage; he snatched a pearl-handled Colt and fired a shot that passed Hatfield and thudded into the corridor wall a few inches from Elsie. The next one might hit her. Forced to shoot, the Ranger could take no chances; the report of his gun echoed Torquila's, the Mexican bandit was taking careful aim to kill his opponent.

As though painted there by a magic, invisible hand, a round, bluish hole appeared between the murderous raider's black eyes. Torquila flopped back on the pillows, the weight of the gun in his hand pulling his arm down to the floor.

Rosa screamed and ran over to the dead man.

"That's two," Hatfield muttered. "Three left: Ross, Number Four, and — the Chief!"

The shooting would bring the guards running, rouse the whole camp. Hatfield grasped Elsie's wrist.

"Ban's outside," he said quickly. Her face was drawn, pale; she recognized him and ran with him, to the back, out the open window. The stamp of feet, yells up front, sounded as rapidly they crossed to the spot where the rope dangled.

"Morton!" Hatfield softly hailed.

Ban peeked over the fence. "Elsie — yuh okay?"

"Yes, Ban, they didn't hurt me much, seemed to be saving me —"

Hatfield swept her up in his powerful arms, soft body a feather in his grip. For a moment he held her and in that moment envied Ban Morton. Women were not for a Ranger, save as passing fancies; he could not ask a woman to share such a dangerous life.

Morton was standing up on Black Rascal. He caught Elsie's shoulders and Hatfield boosted her over the thorny top so Morton could hold her clear.

"Get goin'," ordered Hatfield. "Ride for home and stay there with yore guards, till I come. Don't let the ranchers attack the lumber camp. *Adios.*"

"But yuh — what yuh mean to do?" demanded Ban.

The Ranger looked over his shoulder. Dark figures were leaping up from sleep; others running from the house. "Callate I'll stick here a while. Ride, Morton."

He turned, crouched in the fence shadow,

as a dozen renegades in the lead, whirled toward him. His Colts flashed death into them, ripping their front, throwing confusion into them by accurate firing. Answering slugs of hate plugged into the palings; one nipped his arm, and blood was warm from his cut thigh and flesh; bullets spurted dust around him.

Giving Morton a minute to get started, and smashing the bandits' first charge, Hatfield swung, seized the lariat tied to Goldy's saddle horn. He drew himself to the top and, torn at by the thorns, dropped into the saddle.

Yells raged in the stockade. "After them!" a Mexican voice shrieked.

Leaping on their bucking, shaggy mustangs, the bandits swept pell-mell out of the gates, rounded the corner to run into the blasting gunfire of the Ranger. When they jerked their reins, sliding to a stop, dust billowing under the lashing hoofs, to take steady aim at the hombre who had killed their chief, Hatfield pivoted the golden sorrel and headed west, zigzagging in the chaparral.

The raging mob trailed him, whooping with fury. He made another brief stand, and, drawing them off westward by a clever, calculated chase, kept them fully occupied while Ban Morton and Elsie Ward were riding north for the Rio and Maravilla.

The semi-desert, high mesquite patches casting ebony shadows in the mellow moonlight, was covered by a thick, tangled growth that allowed dodging and hiding; innumerable cattle trails crossed and crisscrossed; with the aromatic odor of the plants in his nostrils, the Ranger led the renegades far into the wilds of the chaparral before he gave Goldy his rein along a winding but well-marked trail northwest. The screeches of his baffled pursuers grew dim as he drew away; now and then he heard the distant pop of a gun as a Mexican fired at a shadow.

He dared not pause; Friday was but two days off and it would take him the best part of one to ride back to the Maravilla country. From what he had overheard and observed at Torquila's hacienda, he knew that a diabolical trap was laid, to murder wholesale the ranchers; and, added to Ross's three hundred killers must be the five hundred bandit warriors heading north on the very trail he was following.

"Hafta split 'em," he muttered, looking back over his shoulder at the sweep of the Mexican wilds.

Though obviously much used, beaten by thousands of hoofs in both directions, this track was rougher than the direct corridor from Torquila's to the Bar W. Control of Ward's spread would permit the raiders on Texas a quicker, easier route on which to run up their forced labor. This way sharp, serrated ridges, like the teeth of a giant's comb, smashed the terrain, dead volcanic country traversed by dry arroyos that would present a troublesome problem to a large outfit. There were rocky passes, so narrow at times that only one horseman could proceed.

Day found him still in the fastnesses of Coahuila. The new light spread over the wilderness. Driving on with the unfailing, terrific power of his body and mind, the Ranger looked back from a rocky mesquite ridge, saw in the south distance blue hills a hundred miles off, the bushed badlands between; and beyond, across the dip in which the Rio Grande ran, the rising soil of Texas, the soil he loved, grown over with heavy chaparral.

The wooded mountains forming the Maravilla watershed were sharply outlined against the vast blue-gray dome of the sky, the western slopes still black with shadow. The steady clop of the sorrel's hoofs on the stony trail never faltered. Birds were up with the sun, insects starting to fly. "Figger this

153

here chief won't leave anything to luck!" he mused, obsessed by the vital necessity of reaching Maravilla in time.

Ahead were half a thousand bandits with their prisoners. As the blood-red sun streamed up on his right he took care that all metal was covered so no reflection might telegraph a warning to the Mexicans — such a flash would be visible for miles. Eyes moving first from the immediate trail sign to the distant sky, he saw a springy cactus plant slowly coming back into position, very slowly, and from such traces he could tell how far up the big band, traveling more slowly than he, might be.

On Hatfield alone rested the hopes of Maravilla, of Texas; he must get through, and swiftly.

Reaching the Rio, in a marshy area he found fresh indentations left by horses and mules, imprints gradually filling with water. He started the sorrel into the warm, sandy-bedded river, and, on the Texas shore, scanned the sky ahead. He was rewarded by several scintillating flashes, like runaway sunbeams, that he knew were caused by the rays striking on metal accoutrements. Pushing on, he observed a flock of crows winging swiftly to the west. Their caws were faint on the warming breeze; but the birds did not fly far, but lighted in a clump of huisache trees.

"Camped," he grunted aloud.

He began to circle, with the careful approach of an Indian stalking prey. An hour later, finding a way through threading cattle trails in the chaparral, he paused on a mesquite ridge to scan the Mexican camp, now to the south as he stood.

They were resting for the day, marching at night; armed renegades in high-peaked hats, their sentinels slouched on their shaggy mustangs, chin on breast, Winchester lying across the saddle horn. In the center the main band slept on their guns, ringing the peon captives; the big herd of horses and mules, with a hundred head of rustled beef cattle from the Circle 5 raid, guarded by skilled vaqueros.

The Lone Wolf shoved north on the beaten track left by former parties of Torquila's raiders driving stolen stock and peons to the Southwest Company's mountain camps; the road was ever up, slow going. Foam flecked the giant sorrel's handsome hide, scratched by thorns; the rider was filmed with alkali dust, and dried blood stained his ripped clothing.

Through the fiery day heat they rode; below, through a leafy vista, Hatfield looked over his shoulder at the vast country of the Big Bend, sheening with wild loveliness in the white-hot sun.

It had been dark again for hours when they reached the stands of live-oak and pine forming the watershed of the Maravilla. The man and rider snatched a brief rest, a drink and a quick meal, off the trail; again, resilient as tempered steel, the Ranger rode on.

He knew there were alert sentries around Valentine Ross's quarters. He cut northeast, passing the spot where he had been chased on his first visit into the hills, and struck the Maravilla below the shacks of the Lumber Company.

Timber had been cut off a local area on both sides of the river; he proceeded cautiously, and, seeing through the trees the ruby-red glow of a cigarette, the night wind soughing in his ears, he dismounted and crept from tree stump to tree stump. In the moonlight piercing through the open space he noted the black bulk of the heavy dam that diverted the Maravilla.

The dam was constructed of great tree trunks fastened crosswise by chains in the stream; its upper face filled in by a twelve-foot breast of broken rock and clay. The flowing water hit this obstruction and swirled north into the canal cut by the lumbermen, thence through the dry arroyo. Through this the lumbermen could float timber miles northeast to the plains where teams could pick it up and carry it to the railroad without hauling across the mountains.

He saw, down below, a few hundred yards from the dam, the licking flames of a bonfire. A silent shadow in the forest, the Ranger wished to finish his survey before dawn; he must uncover the enemy's plans.

Part he already knew: the five hundred Mexican renegades would be on hand to mop up the ranchers. But there was more: a stunning blow that would leave nothing to chance in battle. Four hundred determined cowmen, fighting for their homeland, might defeat eight hundred hired assassins.

It was easy for the expert Ranger to cross the dry bed of the Maravilla below the dam. From a fringe of bushes and trees he looked out upon a large space from which higher growth had been hastily removed. It was as though a great playfield had here been sliced out of the wilderness.

Toward the stream bed, on outcropping bedrock, that bonfire burned, red tongues licking up into the sky, smoke drifting off on the west wind. Crouched on the dried bank, eyes on a level with the fire, the Ranger saw the burly figures of lumberjacks, in corduroy and helmet, as they moved back and forth against the light.

The breeze brought him a whiff of that smoke. The odor was strange, as he sniffed it.

"Glycerine," he mused, "and acid — wood —"

Bit by bit, suspicion turning to certainty in his swift brain, he began to work down, keeping in the river bed, the banks hiding him as he moved. The henchmen of Valentine Ross were alert, and heavily armed; he heard the clang of metal on stones, sounds he recognized as picks and shovels digging deep in the earth. A round stone, disturbed by his weight on the shifty sands, rolled and struck another with a sharp clack.

"What's that?" a snarling voice demanded.

Hatfield froze, a shadow back of the shadow of a great boulder anchored in the river bed. That was Ross's voice, and close at hand. A pistol roared, the flame stabbing straight at his hiding place; the slug spat into the sand, whipped grains into his face, but he did not move the fraction of an inch.

"Jest an animal, Boss," remarked a 'jack.

"Guess so," growled Ross.

The bunch moved off, and Hatfield kept

on. Danger was close; he was some distance from Goldy, and, afoot, might be surrounded and taken once they guessed his presence, or glimpsed his stealthy figure.

He left the ditch outside the fire circle and came up toward the cleared area from the east. Brilliant moonlight illuminated the wide flat space where the 'jacks were finishing up their task. Men moved rapidly to and fro, shoveling dirt and rocks, leveling off; others walked back and forth from the fire, near which stood Valentine Ross and his bodyguard, throwing empty boxes on the blaze.

That acrid fire smoke drifted full into his nose and eyes.

"Dynamite!" he muttered.

That innocent looking space of cleared land was mined, mined by a huge quantity of dynamite that had come packed in the boxes. Some of the impregnating material had oozed through the wrappings to the wood, giving the smoke its distinctive smell.

The evil plan of the Syndicate was now his!

Chapter XI
Wholesale Death

Cold fury gripped Jim Hatfield. Ross meant to lead the ranchers onto that prepared field by a clever draw. The great mine would explode, killing and maiming the main bunch of the cowmen, while the Mexican army and 'jacks wiped up the shattered remnants.

Swarming about him were enemies, he heard their calked, heavy boots thudding the dirt, curses as sweating men finished up the death trap that was to destroy all opposition in Maravilla, give control to the Chief and his criminal Syndicate so that they might raid Texas of her natural wealth.

There was no cover so that he could work in closer; the moonlight was bright in the open, and a threat of grayness was coming into the sky behind him. Hatfield crept back to the dip of the river bed, and, crossing it, waited in the thicker bush.

A messenger came whirling up the slopes

from the east. "Ross! Ross!" Hatfield could hear him shouting.

The dawn was at hand and details began to stand out in the dew-damp air. The Ranger could see the heaving, lathered horse the messenger had ridden up. Valentine Ross snatched a paper from the rider, put his pasty, evil face close to it so he might read it in the dimness.

"Scarface!" bawled Ross, his voice echoing through the forest aisles to the officer's hearing. "Quick! Take the fastest horse we have and ride south!"

South. The Mexicans lay that way, five hundred guerrilla fighters; they might prove an overwhelming force if brought up at the right moment, and he knew he must hold them up if that were possible.

The Ranger faded away, and picked up Goldy, waiting in the bush clump as his master had left him. With that dynamite trap set, Hatfield would not pause in his vital, dangerous work until its awful menace was removed. A ghost rider, he watched and glimpsed Scarface, on a swift gray mustang, crossing the dry Maravilla bed, heading on the trail to Mexico.

Half an hour later, as Scarface rounded a turn on the downgrade south, Jim Hatfield pushed Goldy out onto the trail, the sorrel sliding down the rocky side.

"Scarface!" the Ranger said sharply.

The lean hombre jerked on his rein, the gray dancing sideward to a stop. The messenger's twisted face drew up in terror, and a great gasp heaved his lungs.

"Jim!" he quavered. His eyes were like saucers and he sagged in his saddle. Sheer fright actuated him, he thought he was to die and he dug a spur into the gray's ribs, and whirled the horse against Goldy, who snorted and lashed out with an angry hoof. Scarface had grabbed for his gun, and a shrill squeak issued from his constricted throat.

Hatfield grabbed the gray's bit as the mustang jumped from Goldy's kick; a touch of his knees and the sorrel crushed in. The Ranger yanked back the gray's head, slewing Scarface around so he couldn't shoot. As Scarface fought to come back into firing position, Hatfield hit him across the forearm with his gun barrel.

A sharp crack sounded. With a yelp of anguish, Scarface dropped his pistol from his helpless, numbing hand, and the tall jigger with a cold surety of movement that appalled Scarface, grabbed his prisoner's shoulder, leaped down to the trail, yanking the messenger to earth.

He shook Scarface violently.

"Pass over that note," he snarled viciously.

Utterly cowed, whimpering with the pain of his cracked arm, Scarface's left hand shook as he extracted a paper from inside his shirt and passed it over. "Stand quiet or I'll drill yuh," Hatfield snapped.

Scarface was half sobbing; he held his injured wrist tightly with his left hand. The Ranger glanced at the paper; there was writing on both sides, one in a bold hand that said:

Ross. Make it Thursday morn instead of Friday.

And a hasty scrawl on the other where Ross had dashed it off in pencil, using the same sheet:

Torquila: rush up your men at once.

"Thursday — that's today," growled the Ranger. He stared into the cringing, twisting face of the lanky hombre. "Yuh ain't deliverin' this," he told Scarface. "I know plenty, and there's some things yuh're goin' to tell me; don't try to lie." His voice was an icy stab that seemed to penetrate the miserable captive's heart, for he shivered.

"Who's chief of this dirty bus'ness?"

"Vasco Torquila," Scarface replied instantly.

Hatfield's hand shot out, grasped him by

the scrawny throat; the long, viselike fingers tightened and blood purpled Scarface's cheeks, his eyes bulged from his head.

"Yuh lie," snarled the Ranger.

Scarface was trying to shake his head; Hatfield relaxed his grip a bit, so he could talk: "So help me, that's the truth!" choked Scarface. "Don't kill me, Jim! Torquila gives Ross orders sometimes."

"Not this time. Ross is givin' the orders to Torquila, ain't he? And who sent this note up to Ross, givin' *him* orders?"

"I dunno. There's a guy named Fat Phil in Bowie but yuh kilt him yoreself, Ranger."

"This note come from Bowie?"

"I figger so. The only bosses I know are Phil, Ross and Torquila; they got a political connection but I couldn't say who he is." Scarface's earnestness convinced the Ranger; like most of the rank and file, Scarface was unaware of the identity of the savage chief the Ranger sought.

He pumped Scarface dry, but obtained little more information than he already had ferreted out for himself. The sun was rosy in the blue sky dome as he finished his catechism of the prisoner.

A few miles south the Mexicans were camped, awaiting their orders from Ross. And, very dim, from the northeast sounded a number of faint yet distinctly staccato cracks.

"Gunfire, and heavy," growled the Ranger.

His clawed hand started again for Scarface's throat, his eyes searched the lanky hombre's soul. "That's — that's the ranchers attackin'," gasped Scarface, shrinking from that clutch of steel that shut off his wind and took all the strength out of his muscles.

Hatfield's eyes darkened. They had disobeyed his orders, and were rushing up to stunning, wholesale slaughter. They were rushing into the dynamite trap laid by Valentine Ross.

He snatched the lariat from the gray's saddle, and swiftly bound Scarface, left him gagged and tied to a tree back out of sight of the trail. Forking Goldy, Hatfield rode full-speed back toward the dynamite mine.

Minute after minute passed, minutes of time precious, that meant the life or death of Maravilla, of Texas. The golden sorrel's legs flew at full speed, as the Lone Wolf urged him on, crooning to him a wild song of battle. The great horse dug in his hoofs as he fought on uphill, swinging into the forest south of the Maravilla.

"Got to make it," Hatfield growled, eyes fixed ahead through the leafy vistas. Vines and bushes forced them to swing, zigzag this way and that to get through. The seconds seemed to speed, as the vital time passed.

When he came up on the south side of the Maravilla, below the dam, he could see through the trees a hundred and fifty of the lumbermen, in their brown corduroy and flannel shirts, and helmet caps, down behind the clay banks of the canal. They were heavily armed, with Winchester rifles and spare pistols, boxes of ammunition open and waiting. Eagerly they scanned the eastern bush for the approach of their enemies, the ranchers, running full-speed into certain death.

Four hundred yards below, close to the dry river, were Valentine Ross and half a dozen burly 'jacks, his personal bodyguard. The pasty-faced, green-eyed killer, gulping in fury, watched the east, too, as he squatted among a nest of rocks.

To the north, fifty yards off, the bonfire was dying away, most of the wooden boxes consumed, smoke drifting off on the gentle, sweet west wind. And below, not far from Ross, began the open area purposely cleared, where the great dynamite mine was planted.

The gunfire to the east was terrific, mingling with it in the short lulls the yells of furious cowmen. The defiant shout of Ross's second gang arose, leading on the ranchers, as Hatfield had guessed they would.

Jim Hatfield quickly took in the situation. There was no time to warn the ranchers, stop them; so he headed Goldy down the south bank into the river bed. Digging in his spurs, rising up from the saddle, Hatfield was abreast of Valentine Ross as the great sorrel headed up the north bank.

Down through the bush, Hatfield glimpsed the attacking citizens of Maravilla. Riding in full battle array, the ranchers were well-armed; in the van he recognized young Ban Morton's slim figure on Black Rascal. There were other leaders, the Bar W waddies, among them Shorty and Arizonny, and men from the Circle 5, fighting hombres drawn from every outfit within two hundred miles of Bowie. Four hundred splendid young men, the heart of Maravilla, were riding up to drive out the murderers who sought to ruin their home range.

One hundred and fifty mounted lumbermen were slowly retreating before the spirited onslaught of the cowmen. The 'jacks fought a smart, drawing action, feigning to stand, then running on back up the slopes toward the dynamite mine. Men and animals were being hit on both sides, though the rough ground, the motion of jolting beasts made close aim difficult.

Valentine Ross squatted in his pile of rocks, and in his left hand he held a matchbox. In his right Hatfield could see, in the bright yellow sunlight, the white match stick with red-and-blue tip, that the boss had ready to strike. Hatfield's eyes were on a level with the ground, as he came up from the river bed; through the heavy fringe along the Maravilla he glimpsed Ross's pasty face, green eyes shining with a tigerish glow, as Ross looked around.

"Huntin' for them Mexes," Hatfield muttered. "He's at the fuse end."

The bunch of 'jacks leading the ranchers to death was at the east edge of the mined area. Hot curses and hotter gunfire ripped the cowmen, blinded by the fury of the fight and their long pent-up hatred for the destroyers.

No shouted warning could reach to the ranchers in such a din, and no time remained to tell them what they were riding into. Above, back of the clay banks beyond the canal, lurked the second half of the lumbermen, waiting in ambush to wipe up any possible survivors of that terrible explosion.

"It's the only thing to do," Hatfield mused.

He had sized up the danger-fraught, fatal situation at a glance, knew he had but a half minute in which to strike. Then Ross would be surrounded by the 'jacks coming in from the east. Hatfield knew that what he attempted was practically suicide but he had no choice. Unless he could seize that scant time-fraction it was all over for Maravilla, even for Texas!

Squatted low with his ready match to strike and light the fuse at the proper instant, Ross looked like the devil himself. His white, slim hand — a dude's hand — would touch off the wholesale murder.

The golden sorrel's hoofs dug into the sandy north bank of the river bed, kicking back loose rocks, the noises drowned in the battle din. Jim Hatfield urged Goldy through the bushes.

Ross could not fail; squatted at the gray connection to the tremendous mine, he would time the death stroke perfectly. He was ringed by half a dozen big 'jacks, his guard and the rocks helped protect him from any long shot the Ranger might try.

As Hatfield, low over the golden sorrel, touched Goldy with a spur, the horse lunged out from the screen of bush. At that moment, Valentine Ross looked impatiently back over his shoulder again, for Torquila's men.

Ross saw the tall jigger as Hatfield whirled straight at him. At sight of his arch-enemy, Ross gulped and uttered a shriek of astounded rage, pointing at the tall rider galloping in. The 'jacks with him had their eyes glued on the fight below, and they swung at his warning, threw up their rifles as Hatfield opened fire with both Colts.

His bullets thudded into the flesh and bone of the men grouped around Ross.

"Kill him! Kill him!" screamed Ross, vitriol of fury burning his slender throat.

The seconds fleeted. Each one brought the bunching ranchers nearer the trap, upon that ripping, tearing death.

Two of the men shielding Ross fell at the first blasting volley of the Ranger's guns. He let go again, and the bullets tore an arc of death along the small group of 'jacks. The terrible accuracy of his fire, the grim, rugged face of the great fighting man, appalled them; he was almost upon them, and still he rode hell-for-leather straight into what seemed certain death.

Slugs from their rattled guns whirled about the Ranger's head and body; one missed him by inches, another tore the saddle and cut Goldy's hide. The sorrel gave a tremendous bound forward, shoulder knocking down a lumberman, his rider's guns flaming the end for a fourth and fifth. The sixth man with Ross turned with a scream of terror and ran off in mad retreat, arms over his face.

Hatfield left his saddle in a flying leap as Valentine Ross, dropping the box and match, snatched out his small-caliber pistol and aimed at the Ranger. Ross fired point-blank at the moving officer. The lead hit Hatfield as he traveled through the air, pierced between the tendons of his neck and shoulder, stinging with horrid anguish. Then his spurred boots struck Ross in the stomach, knocked him flat as the Ranger's weight came through.

Hatfield's hand found the green-eyed hombre's scrawny throat. He held the furious chief, writhing like a six-foot rattler, in a grip of steel, and banged Ross's head against the jagged rocks until the blood flowed scarlet from the smashed scalp.

A fraction of a minute remained; he knew that, even as he fought Ross for control of that great mine. To kill Ross would not stop the slaughter; the incoming lumberjacks would light the fuse as they came from the open space. And the bunch above, across the canal, had seen the Ranger as he attacked Ross in a mad swirl of power.

The golden sorrel gave a sharp warning whinny, seized his master's shirt in his teeth and shook. From above, the lumbermen in ambush were starting across the canal, and their bullets were rapping into the rocks, close to the Ranger, though they dared not shoot too close for fear of killing the prostrate Ross.

Ross relaxed under him; Hatfield snatched up the match box, struck a match and touched the flickering flame to the gray fuse. It sputtered bluish sparks, took hold with a low, swishing sound. The gray line grew rapidly black as the fire ran swiftly along it.

Like the jaws of a giant pincers the two bodies of lumbermen were closing upon Hatfield. The gang leading the ranchers on was now over the mined space.

"Look out, he's lit the fuse!" That shriek, shrill with terror, came from the mob bearing downhill on the officer.

Hatfield whirled, guns spitting death into their bunched ranks. Suddenly they all saw that faintly smoking, blue-sparked train to hell, and with precipitate haste they turned and fled for cover. The 'jacks on the mined area, deafened by gunfire, backs to the rocks, did not realize the fuse was lighted.

Only a few happened to turn, and realize the import, but it was too late.

Eyes staring in horror, they tried to point to the running flame. With horror-gripped eyes they followed the spark that would touch off the percussion caps attached to the dynamite.

The Ranger leaped to Goldy; the explosion might kill, so close were they to the mighty mine. He was stopped as a clawlike hand clutched his booted ankle, tripped him; Ross made his final play, trying to take his arch-foe along.

Even as he fell, weight taken on his outstretched left hand, the Ranger twisted his body around, lashed at Ross's face with his Colt. The sharp sight cut down across the green eyes that flamed with hatred. He raised his thumb from the hammer and Valentine Ross let go, fell back on the jagged rocks, head a bloody horror.

Hatfield scrambled to his feet. Only instants remained; he hit the saddle in a single bound, and Goldy, seeming to guess the danger, leaped with tremendous strides for the depression of the river bed. The sorrel flew over the brink, sliding and half turning on the steep downslope. At that moment the whole universe exploded, and horse and rider were knocked flat, rolling over and

over across the rocky dry course of the Maravilla.

Chapter XII
A Ghost Rides

Hatfield's next impression was that he was caught in a terrific cloudburst, a heavy downpour that spat upon the leaves and sand.

Yet the drops were stinging, hurt as they struck his head and body; he put his arms over his head as he lay flat in the stream bed. He realized that it was not water that was falling but a violent hail of stones, dirt and rubble. There were worse things than inanimate matter in that rain: arms and legs, parts of the bodies of men and animals.

After seconds that dragged interminably the worst of the downpour ceased, spattering off as smaller fragments landed. He sat up, shook himself, fighting off the stunned blackness that the shattering dynamite had brought over the world.

His vision was obscured by a giant smoke pall drifting into the brilliant heavens. The biting odor of the discharged explosive was in his flared nostrils as he came up on his knees, rocking from side to side as his equilibrium returned. His face was bloody from abrasions caused by jagged flints, and his skin blackened by powder and dirt.

Goldy was scrambling to his feet; the golden sorrel's eyes were as wide as saucers, flaming red. He pawed furiously at the sand and rocks, kicked out wildly at the leg of a man that had fallen on his back, the dismembered limb strangely clothed in corduroy with hobnail boot intact.

"That did it," muttered Hatfield aloud, but his voice was lost in the banging of his shattered eardrums. No living creature could stand near such an explosion, nor bear it without terrific shock.

Then, over the mighty wilderness, a brooding quiet reigned. Life seemed to suspend animation for minutes, eerie time interval that was unbearably long.

Pulling himself together, shaking his head in an effort to clear his hearing, Hatfield slowly stepped over to Goldy and touched the quivering gelding's velvet arched neck. The horse quieted under his hand, and the Ranger led him up the north bank and mounted.

Now he could look, through the clearing drifts of smoke and dirt, upon what had been the cleared area wherein Valentine Ross had planted his gigantic dynamite mine. A raw, bleeding crater, many yards in depth, showed there, the entire earth blasted away to bedrock and clay. Nothing remained of the lumberjacks who had been standing on top of the mine, only fragments with here and there an entire corpse, killed with the brutal vagaries of the explosive.

He wiped his stinging eyes with the back of his long hand, and his gaze sought the spot below where the ranchers had been coming. The explosion had stunned them all, and several had been injured by flying rocks, but the main army had been spared, saved by the Ranger's play. Horses were rising up, and riders, thrown from the saddle, were on their feet, rocking dizzily from shock.

Jim Hatfield picked out young Ban Morton's slim figure, and he started down toward them, skirting the crater of death. Sounds of life once more rose over the Maravilla wilderness: birds were flying off in the brilliant sky, and the excited voices of the cowmen were audible to his quieting eardrums.

Then someone opened fire on him, the bullet spanging into the clay side of the crater. Looking back, he saw that the 'jacks beyond the canal had come to life and were shooting again. He drew a Colt and rattled them down behind their breastwork as his slugs spat up flies of clay where they peeked over the embankment.

Morton recognized Jim Hatfield as the tall jigger pushed Goldy among the massed ranchers. Some were more dazed than others, running their hands over their faces as though the skin were brittle and might break, eyes round as circles, breath fast. Coughs and sneezes from dust-clogged throats, and the monotonous cursing of a nerve-shattered waddy broke the quiet.

"Jim! Jim!" Morton croaked hoarsely, spitting out dust.

"Howdy, Ban," the Ranger told him. He was rolling a cigarette, and lit it as he coolly scanned the faces of the cowmen, turning toward him. Silently, they began to gather about Hatfield and Morton, and their eyes, meeting his, fell before his stern gaze.

"How is it," Hatfield drawled, "yuh come up here, gents? I left orders yuh was to stay put till yuh heard from me."

The sunlight gleamed on the rugged fighting jaw of Jim Hatfield; and it glinted back from the silver star, set on a silver circle, emblem of the Texas Rangers, pinned to his vest.

"Ranger! That big jigger's a Texas Ranger!" The whispered exclamation traveled like wildfire through the great crowd.

"I knowed it, we oughta guessed," a cowman growled. "Nobody could ride and fight like that 'cept a Ranger!"

Suddenly a hoarse cheer welled from them as they shouted for the hombre who had saved them. Hatfield, modest as he was courageous, raised a hand to quell the ovation.

"Nobody could stop 'em comin' up, Jim," cried Morton. "I was close to home, bringin' Elsie up from Torquila's, when I met the whole parcel, four hunderd men, ravin' for the hills. Word had gone out Ward was murdered and Elsie kidnaped; yuh know Ogalvie was killed and Keith bad wounded by Ross when he raided Bowie. So's Mayor Yager hurt, so bad he can't ride.

"Every man who could be spared from the ranches took up his guns and started; Senator Ardmore was so riled he advised 'em to attack the lumbermen and drive 'em out, though he's always been for lawful means afore. Yager ordered 'em to go ahaid and so'd Keith. I done told 'em all yuh said, that yuh was okay and had saved Elsie and Ward, but they jest kept a-comin' all the same."

Marshal Alf Betts, the little old town offi-cer of Bowie, wooden leg sunk in the soft earth, frowned up at the tall Ranger.

"I'm for cleanin' out that nest of snakes," he growled.

Shorty, from the Bar W, drawled, "Lucky for us that dynamite went off when it did."

Ban Morton was staring at Hatfield. "You — you set it off, Jim, and saved us," he shouted. "So that's what they had planned; it was a trap, to lead us up here and blow us all to hell!"

Hatfield shrugged. The ranchers, watching the mighty Ranger, suddenly realized that he alone had preserved them. Another cheer split the warm air.

Hatfield was regarding Marshal Betts, with a deliberation that made the small hombre shift uncomfortably. Betts cried, "That's so, Mister; I got a telegram for yuh."

He reached inside his shirt, pulled out a yellow envelope. The Ranger took it, and scanned the message, written in a careful hand.

It was a reply to his wire, dispatched by the deceased Sheriff Godey's messenger:

"Southwest Lumber Co. lease okay and legal. Prevent citizens from attacking. Take no drastic steps till you hear from me. McDowell."

The gray-green eyes darkened; then a puzzled light fleeted in them. "Huh," he mused. "Sounds like the captain's gettin' soft. Hell, no, he couldn't be, not that old tiger!" He swung again on Betts.

"Look, Marshal. One or two things I wanta know: who told yuh to jog Shorty's mem'ry that day at the Bar W? And who give yuh this message to hand me?"

Betts scratched his sunburned, bald head. The Ranger, carefully observing the watered blue eyes, decided that while they did not show much intelligence they were honest. "Why," the marshal replied, "come to think, it was Senator Ardmore who told me he'd heard yuh was the man snatched Scarface from the boys. And the senator's a mighty good man and a powerful help to the community. It was him figgered this telegram must be fer you; I asked around, seein' as how Godey's man, the sheriff bein' daid, left the message at Jack's saloon."

Winchester bullets, at long range were plopping into the dirt and bush from above the canal; the remaining lumbermen had taken cover behind the clay banks.

"Hafta clean them out fust of all," remarked the Ranger, tossing away the stub of his cigarette. "Load up, gents."

As the unwounded members of the vigilantes swiftly checked pistols and rifles, shoved fresh shells into empty chambers, and pacified the alarmed, wide-eyed mustangs, Hatfield drew Ban Morton to one side.

"Take that black horse of yores and ride fast as yuh kin to Lenox. Ask the telegraph operator to give yuh copies of all telegrams sent by Captain McDowell from Austin."

Morton hated to quit the battle but he could not disobey the Ranger. He swung Black Rascal and with a wave of his hand the bronc buster lined out northeast down the slopes.

"C'mon," ordered Hatfield, as the ranchers gathered before him, ready to dig in. "We'll wipe up that gang."

He led the way, skirting the crater of destruction. The lumbermen's bullets were rapping closer as Goldy snorted and stepped over the corpse of Valentine Ross, ripped by rocks, doubled into a constricted shape, lying sixty feet from the rock nest where the fuse end had been hidden.

"That'll be Number Three in that Syndicate," the Ranger thought.

He swung toward the dry Maravilla, the

cowmen bunching at his heels, shooting back at the 'jacks. His keen eyes, traveling from right to left, looking over the debris, suddenly stopped. The explosion had blown the bonfire to pieces; the blackened circle of earth showed where it had been. And there were several pieces of the wooden boxes of which it had been composed; one was nearly intact and a corrugation came across the bronzed forehead of the Ranger.

"Huh," he muttered aloud.

A bullet bit a chunk from his Stetson crown; he knew there was work to be done, and quickly. It was possible that the explosion and heavy firing would bring up the Mexican army, and he wanted to deal with the lumbermen separately; his strategy had split the two armies.

Hatfield went across the Maravilla and worked up through the forest. They did not stop till they were above the position of the entrenched 'jacks.

"Flanked 'em," bawled Marshal Betts, throwing up his old horse pistol which boomed like a small cannon in the shadowed sweet air of the woods.

From partial cover they raked the line of lumbermen. The heavy gunfire from the cowmen tore into the now unprotected 'jacks, rolling them up; they fought to get behind one another, and they were disheartened and shocked at the terrible loss of their leaders and mates. Scattered shots came back, as the remnant of Ross's once powerful band stood hesitantly before the charge of their enemies.

"Bust that dam right now," bawled Hatfield, and he sent two hundred cowmen to clean up the 'jacks, who had broken and started running.

A loud cheer rose, as the remaining ranchers set about pulling down the dam that diverted the precious water of the Maravilla. Once the break was made the water assisted, swirling through the holes and carrying rocks and clay, turning aside the big logs.

Up on the north bank of the river, the ranchers watched the stream going back into its proper channel. And then, from the south side, among the thick bush and trees, a tremendous fusillade of bullets whirled at them. A half dozen ranchers were hit, before the Ranger's mighty voice penetrated to them, ordering them to hunt cover.

Turning on this new threat, they saw among the trees over the Maravilla, riding with the mad abandon of their race, half a thousand Mexican bandidos, charging with hot cries of hate upon them.

"Torquila! Torquila!" a cowman shrilled.

Jim Hatfield, pushing up erect in his stirrups, stared at the charging Mexes. In the van rode a giant figure, dark face smudged by mustache and goatee, a black cape wrapped about his body, peaked hat strapped low over his flashing eyes.

Vasco Torquila led the bandit charge.

CHAPTER XIII
NUMBER FOUR

Taking advantage of tree trunks, of huge boulders and piles of cut logs left by the lumbermen, the dismounted ranchers opened up on the bandits. The Mexican charge came to the brink of the muddy river, still carrying debris and clay as it rode eastward.

Hatfield was trying to pick off the chieftain, but the swift movements, the rising dust and smoke, intervening bodies of Mexicans, spoiled his chances. The other bunch of cowmen, hearing the new shooting from the river bank, left the scattered fugitives running for the tall bush and returned, whooping it up, to the fight. At sight of them the renegades faltered; the odds were nearly even, and the ranchers had a protected position.

For minutes the Mexicans fought bravely, but their ranks were bitten into by the accurate hard-shooting cowmen. A hundred were hit to twenty ranchers; the Texans roared in triumph, fever heat of battle flushing sweated, stained faces. Mad with victory, at the fierce joy that is the thrill of revenge, they jumped up at Hatfield's order and charged through the running water of the river.

The charge sent the wavering bandits back. As Hatfield, shoving the dripping Goldy up the south bank, swung to hunt the giant leader of the foe, he glimpsed Torquila as the chief galloped hell-for-leather south among the trees.

Between his position and the fleeing Torquila interposed the main body of the bandits. The cowmen charged, and Torquila's hombres, having failed to find a bloody, shattered remnant of Texans to clean up, knew they had run into a hornet's nest of hell. The flight of their leader broke them altogether; every Mexican swung to escape, horses bumping, piling up. Utter rout followed, and the ranchers attacked them viciously, taking prisoners, shooting those who resisted.

For mile after mile, picking off the bunches of bandits, leaving dead, wounded or prisoners, the victorious vigilantes raged south. They reached the camp of the Mexicans, where the new bunch of peons was held under a skeleton guard that fled in alarm at sight of the disastrous rout.

Hatfield freed the captives. To several of the more intelligent he gave advice: to get in touch with the Mexican rurales and inform the police of Torquila's perfidy. With the main band smashed, the rurales could clean up the hacienda, and break the power of the bandits.

His gray-green eyes hunted from corpse to corpse, from batch of prisoners to batch of prisoners, for that big rider. But the chief, mounted on a fast, fresh horse, had faded away, disappeared.

Worn out, torn and blood-stained, but filled with jubilant emotion, the ranchers straggled back at dusk to the mountain camp of the Southwest Lumber Company. Wounded men had staggered up here, and prisoners were being collected. They were turned into the stockade from which the miserable Mexican slaves were released. Hatfield saw to it that the peons were provided with mounts and food for their journey home.

In Ross's shack he found that map that had told him much of the Syndicate's plans. He smoothed it out and looked at the vast territory that had been in their plans. He put it in his pocket, its significance entirely clear to him.

"Hafta take him," he mused, as he watched the ranchers setting fire to the shacks, destroying the enemy camp. "An hombre who could get up such a scheme can figure out others!"

His power and skill had saved Maravilla; but he knew he was far from through. Texas must take the perpetrator of the wholesale horrors that threatened to engulf her.

Dawn found him down below, near the spot where the dead bonfire had burned. Young Ban Morton, riding a lathered and heaving Black Rascal, pushed up to Hatfield as the Ranger curiously looked over the half of the wooden box he had noted the previous day.

"Here's yore message," Morton reported; he was covered with dust and his face was drawn, from his hard ride. Curiously, he stared at the wooden container, its edges scarred with black. "What yuh got, Jim?"

In the clear light, Ban could see that the box end contained bits of sawdust; and when Hatfield ran his fingers along the inner wood they came away shining with an oily substance.

"Dynamite was packed in this," the Ranger drawled. "And — I've seen these boxes before, Ban."

He accepted the telegram copy Morton held out. Quickly he scanned it, and his eyes lightened.

"I'll be ridin'," Hatfield told Ban.

"Can I go with yuh?"

"Yeah, if yuh can keep up."

Leaving the main body of ranchers, Hatfield and Morton headed eastward down the slopes.

Another night was on Bowietown, which looked like a deserted village with most of its citizens out, up in the hills to fight the lumbermen, as Jim Hatfield and Ban Morton, ahead of the main army, dismounted in the tree-shaded plaza, with its little speakers' stand empty in the darkness.

They had stopped at the Bar W on their way, for Ban to change horses, for Black Rascal was done in from the hard run to the railroad and back, and also to make certain that Elsie Ward and Sam were in no danger.

The settlement was quiet; the saloons and Yager's store were open but only a few oldsters, too crippled to ride far, were around. Every able-bodied man, save for skeleton guards to hold the ranches, had headed for the west mountains to drive out the invaders. Punchers wounded in the early stages of the fight had straggled back home, and brought news of the cowmen's victory.

Hatfield, Ban Morton limping at his side, made a swift survey of the store and saloons.

"That big place is Senator Ardmore's, Jim," Morton remarked. "Yuh said yuh wanted to talk to him."

The Ranger stared at the square mansion, pretentious for a Western town, standing back in a cut lawn planted with trees and flowers, enclosed by a picket fence.

Dark shadows rested around the gloomy building; at the rear a light gleamed yellow in the kitchen windows. The rest of the house was dark, shades drawn.

"Don't look like the senator's home," exclaimed Ban. "Reck'n Mayor Yager would help us; he was wounded bad when Ross raided his store, though he can walk and talk some."

"We'll try the senator first," Hatfield drawled.

He pulled back the gate and strolled along a gravel walk, rimmed by flowering shrubs and ornamental cactus plants. Wounds stiff and aching from the terrific pace at which he had been going, Hatfield could not yet ease up.

There was work to do, for though the armies of the bandits and lumberjacks had been smashed, the evil brain which ani-

191

mated them still rode free, and Texas would never be safe until the chief of that criminal Syndicate was dead or arrested. Such an hombre, Hatfield was aware, could easily start again; tools were plentiful.

Eyes watching the shadows from side to side, Hatfield went quietly around the square house to the kitchen. He rapped on the door with the butt of his Colt.

"Who's there?" a gruff voice demanded, after a moment.

The Ranger nudged Morton and Ban replied, "It's me, Ban Morton."

"What yuh want?"

"Tell the senator I wanta see him."

"He ain't here. Started for Austin this afternoon."

The Ranger tried the knob but it was locked.

"Open up," he ordered.

"Go 'way. Yuh can't come in."

Shoulder to the panel, the Ranger shoved. A bolt pulled out of its socket and the wood groaned and squeaked, then the whole side gave way and Hatfield stepped into the kitchen.

A man in a rusty black suit, evidently a cast-off of his master's, scowled and swore at them angrily.

"What's the idee," he growled, "bustin' in here?"

But his eyes fell under Hatfield's cool look. The Ranger brushed him aside, strolled through the hall and glanced into the big living room. It was dark, empty, but a closed door to one side attracted him and he tried it, found it locked, no one answered his call, so he shouldered it in.

A wide bedroom opened before him. He saw the white of the counterpane on a tester bed in the middle of the chamber. The curtains were down save for one that looked out on the front walk; that was up a few inches, a lighter space under the shade, as though it had been used to peek through.

Hatfield struck a match; on the bed lay a lank figure. The tall jigger touched his flame to the black wick of a candle standing on a bureau and the little light came up.

The long man on the bed was covered to his triangular chin by a sheet. His mop of iron-gray crisp hair was wildly awry on the pillow, and his body was rigid, sunken eyes wide.

"What's the meaning of this intrusion, sir?" Senator Rathburn Ardmore angrily demanded. "How dare you force your way into my private chamber?"

"Senator," broke in the officer, "I don't

like botherin' yuh since yuh've rode to Austin, but there's one or two things I wanta know. Yuh told Marshal Betts to prod Shorty at the Bar W on me bein' the man who snatched Scarface from the rope."

"You did," Ardmore snapped.

"How yuh knowed it is what interests me. But this telegram haunts me more. Listen: here's the one yuh give Betts to hand me, 'case that dynamite blast yuh so handily didn't go near failed to kill us."

Hatfield nodded at Ban Morton, who took up a position at the hall door, on guard. The Ranger read the fake wire, ordering him to give the Southwest Lumber Company a free hand.

"Now," he went on, "this is the real wire that come to Lenox for me: 'Southwest Lumber lease forged. Only granted limited cutting permit in small area north of Maravilla. On your advice traced money paid for incoming timber to Austin office of Senator Rathburn Ardmore of Bowie. Rumors in capital Ardmore has offered bribes to members of legislature for support in obtaining leases on other public resources of Texas. Clean up Maravilla. I stand behind you all the way to hell and back. McDowell.' "

The thin man in the bed trembled violently; his strange, bony face contorted, flushed a deep purple.

"Get out," he shouted. "Get out! You can talk to my attorney, sir. Leave my home at once."

Hatfield shifted closer, steel fingers seizing the bony arm hidden under the covers. The circling grip held Ardmore helpless; Hatfield took a small pistol from his hand, as he pulled the senator's arm into view.

"Yuh ain't got the nerve to use thet," the Ranger drawled.

"Don't — don't!" whispered Ardmore, suddenly cracking as the gray-green eyes drilled deep into his soul. He was a physical coward and the pain of the hold shook him; plainly he was under a great mental strain.

"Callate yuh're Number Four," Hatfield told him. "Number Four in the Syndicate to raid Texas. Yuh ain't got the murderer's nerve yore chief has." His voice turned suddenly harsh, terrifying; Ardmore jumped nervously: "Talk, and talk fast, Ardmore. Yuh want to hang by the neck?"

The senator moaned, writhed, "I — I only handled the legal end, Ranger. I swear it. I never shot anybody."

"Not even Ward?" asked Hatfield grimly. "I seen the rock pile where he was wounded."

"Why, I wasn't even up there that day! *He*

195

shot him during the battle!" He broke off with a gasp. "He'll kill me," he yelled, reddened eyes bulging with tenor.

Papers rustled in the Ranger's hand. "See this map? These letters mark the natural resources of southwest and central Texas, timber, coal and iron. The man who made it wrote this fake message to me."

Again his steel fingers closed on the wincing senator's bony wrist; it was a battle between two fears for Ardmore, fear of the cold, tall officer who had caught up with them, and dread of the hidden chief. The former won.

"I'll talk," Ardmore cried, "I'll tell you everything, Ranger! He forced me to give Betts that message for you, to slow you up; all we needed was a little time to get that timber out of the hills, win a fortune with which to finance our Syndicate."

"And who," Hatfield drawled, "is yore chief? Callate I can say now myself, but I want yore evidence."

Ardmore gulped, as Hatfield leaned ominously toward him again. "He's —" he said quickly.

"Watch it," shouted Ban Morton from the door.

Hatfield was already in action. The slight sound at the window where the curtain was up a few inches, had warned him.

His Colt was out and rising as he whirled in a crouch, on the balls of his feet. The boom of guns roared in the confined space of the room, window glass shattering as the muzzle of a double-barreled shotgun was thrust through. Hatfield had let go at the window as a bunch of unscattered slugs tore into Ardmore's chest, ripping him wide open, the blood spattering the tall jigger.

CHAPTER XIV
CHIEF OF THE SYNDICATE

The second load from the shotgun fanned within an inch of Hatfield's moving head as he went down on one knee for better aim. The vicious whir of the bunched shot passed him, slugged into the wall, bringing down a rain of plaster.

An instant later Ban Morton swept the candle from the bureau, plunging the room in darkness. Glass smashed in other windows; there were gunmen outside, and they began shooting into the room from three angles. Bullets hit the floor, the walls, and the furniture.

"Lie down flat, Ban," called Hatfield.

He drew his second Colt, covering one window after another with lead. The heavy flashes of the guns blinded them; Morton was shooting from the floor.

Hatfield came up on his toes and started like a panther for the door, to get outside and take the hombres attacking. But loud yells, the drumming of hundreds of hoofs, sounded over the din around Ardmore's home. The gunmen outside quit, and as Hatfield crossed to a window and looked out, he glimpsed several dark figures scurrying away, leaping on waiting horses.

When Morton and the Ranger emerged, the assailants had escaped, mingling with the great army of ranchers returning in triumph from the hills. The shouting, victorious cowmen fired their guns into the air, roared with victory.

Bonfires of empty boxes and brush were lighted in the plaza; the platform, weathered by sun and rain, was framed in the red glow. Gleaming faces showed as the cowmen began to whoop it up. Saloons overflowed, hungry and thirsty citizens tanking up.

Senator Ardmore was dead, the shotgun blast having torn his heart. John Ogalvie was dead, and Sam Ward lay wounded at home, as did George Keith; Mayor Smiley Yager, pale and shaky from a head wound, around which a bandage was tightly bound, appeared, supported by two friends.

The citizens gathered about the platform. Yager was the only one of their old leaders present, though there were many lieutenants. Alf Betts took the floor, thumping the creaking boards with his wooden stump.

"Gents," shouted the marshal, "we've beat the lumbermen and Torquila too. Maravilla's safe."

A mighty cheer echoed across the plaza. Alf Betts stumped over, assisted Mayor Yager to rise; the mayor leaned on Bett's arm, smiling cheerily at his people.

Yager's voice was weak but silence fell on them as he began to talk. Jim Hatfield, at the front, stared up into the bluff face.

"Boys," Yager began, "you did it and I'm proud of you. They near finished us, but we've won. I was always in favor of hittin' em and hittin' hard, and that proved to be the right way."

They cheered him. Yager grinned out at his friends. "I heard some of how it was done," he went on. "Texas Ranger Hatfield here, from Austin, saved you from being blown to hell. We're mighty grateful to him and he deserves a yell."

A shout went up for the Ranger. The tall jigger put a spurred boot on the platform and stood beside Yager. The people quieted as they stared at the majestic officer; his eyes were dark as he faced them, easily. Hatfield was not a man to talk much but what he said counted.

"Gents," he began, voice hardly raised yet penetrating to every ear, "there's still some things left undone. Five men formed a Syndicate to take over our natural resources and ruin Texas. They started with Maravilla. That timber up there was the quickest way to pick up a million dollars to finance 'em. Their plans was big, to raid coal, iron, oil and other natural wealth through the state.

"Torquila was one, and he supplied cheap labor, runnin' up peons wholesale; they wanted a corridor to fetch 'em along, and Maravilla, 'specially the Bar W, was it. Fat Phil, the gambler, Torquila, Senator Ardmore, Valentine Ross — they're all gone, 'cept the chief of this vile Syndicate.

"You ranchers was in the way and they tried to wipe yuh out; enough dynamite to blow up a mountain was sent for, but they couldn't bring it through yore waddies. It might have been exploded by bullets. So it was switched here to Bowie, and that was why Ross made that raid: to pick up that dynamite."

Spellbound they listened to his crystal-clear exposé. "Why how could Ross do that?" Yager asked.

"That dynamite was boxed and ready only it wasn't marked as such," Hatfield replied smoothly. "I found one of the boxes it come in, one that didn't altogether burn up. Morton's holdin' it. Bring it here, Ban, and let 'em see for themselves."

Hatfield's weight rested on his left leg; he half turned from the people, as Morton shouldered through the crowd, that opened a way for him. Ban handed up the half-burned box the Ranger had brought down from the hills.

"I seen the boxes the night of Ross's raid, gents," explained Hatfield, "so I got suspicious when I came on this one. Though it's marked 'Canned Tomatoes' it's been packed with sawdust, to cushion the dynamite; some of the oil oozed out, too." Beside the box, Ban Morton handed the Ranger a pair of stuffed saddlebags.

"These here bags belong to the chief who run this shebang," continued the Ranger. He opened the bags, drew forth a folded silk Mexican cape. "Torquila's," he growled. There was a vial with dark liquid in it: "Berry juice to stain his face. And some glue and a mustache and goatee of horsehair, to stick on. This here sombrero is so fine made it kin be folded into a small ball, to stuff in the bag, too.

"Gents, Torquila could hit two places at once because there was *two* of him. The real one, the Mexican bandit leader, and a second, who rode in the dark fixed up like Torquila. Nobody knowed, 'cept the Syndicate; even the Mexes didn't savvy who this second Torquila was — the two-faced snake who shot Sam Ward in the side, up there that day, for Ward wasn't hit by a bullet from in front."

From the back of the spellbound crowd, a gun suddenly flashed its roar. The Ranger staggered as a bullet ripped through his black hair, creased his scalp; a trickle of blood showed on his bronzed forehead, running into his eye.

Pandemonium broke. The dry-gulcher, a dark-browned hombre in cowboy garb, was seized as he tried to reach a horse; in an instant he was knocked down and the furious mob tore at him.

Hatfield whirled, as Mayor Yager flipped his big body backward off the platform, landing in the mêlée. The Ranger's Colt was out but Marshal Betts was on his feet, and stood between. A slug from Yager's pistol, fired from behind the platform, tore a chunk from the officer's left arm as he jumped after the mayor, who had so suddenly thrown off his weakness.

Through the stamping mob, ducked low, Smiley Yager tore a way. Hatfield was after him, watching for a chance to shoot without hurting any excited citizens. Yager reached a clump of oaks, leaped on a great black stallion, dug in his spurs.

The Ranger, coming to the outer circle of the mob, as yet unaware of their mayor's perfidy, whistled three shrill blasts. A few moments later Goldy came galloping up, and Hatfield hit the saddle, whirling south in pursuit of his quarry, the chief of the Syndicate.

Yager was two hundred yards ahead; he swung to shoot back at his lone pursuer, the flashes of his gun spitting his hate for the man who had caught up with him. The Maravilla intervened; Yager's horse, cruelly goaded, bounded down the bank into the current.

Yager turned in midstream to shoot again at the big jigger inexorably shoving after him. Hatfield, the stream licking his thighs, held himself in steel control, fighting off the weakness of wounds and the pace he had undergone for days.

"That's him, shore as hell's hot!" he muttered.

Before him rode the man who had raided the Maravilla range in the guise of Vasco Torquila, at the same time posing as a loyal leader of the ranchers, mayor of their capitol. Driven by the mad lust for wealth and power, Yager had broken every law of decency and of Texas.

A bullet hit the water close to the swimming sorrel; another bit Hatfield's shoulder. Yager's horse was at the south bank, scrambling up. The black slipped as Hatfield's answering slugs rapped rocks and dirt into his glaring eyes.

Close upon his foe, Hatfield threw himself bodily from the saddle, clutched at Yager's leg, yanking the burly mayor from his leather seat. The two big men locked, slipped on the slimy bank, rolled into the water. Hatfield's fingers sought the beating throat of his thrashing, powerful adversary.

The Ranger twisted his lithe body on top; the mayor went down under the surface, but the slippery mud coating Hatfield's hands helped break his grip as Yager fought with the mad desperation of the drowning.

Yager broke free, lashing up, boots digging into the bed of the river. Then he fell back, hand still gripping his Colt, stood there thigh-deep in the running water, and as the mayor's gun covered him, Hatfield raised his thumb off his own hammer.

Yager's slug hit the water a foot in front of Hatfield; the mayor staggered, a black blotch on his furious, twisted brow, from which the bandage had come, showing no injury. Then Yager lost all volition, splashed down, under the surface of the Maravilla.

The Ranger waded slowly toward him, got hold of the limp body, and towed it to the bank.

Captain Bill McDowell stared at the tall Ranger, reporting at Austin Headquarters.

"So yuh got all five," he growled. "And that skunk Mayor Yager was chief of this Syndicate?"

"Yes, sir. It was Yager's plan." Hatfield laid the stained map he had taken from Ross's suitcase on the captain's desk. "He had the natural wealth of Texas marked out, Cap'n. Meant to get a fortune quick by sellin' that timber to put the scheme through. Plenty of cheap labor was to be had in Mexico.

"This Yager posed as a hearty, good feller, but all the time he was workin' underground, and ridin' as Torquila. Yager and Ardmore held back them complaints to us; Yager's spies was all around, and he knowed ev'ry move the ranchers made. It was Yager egged 'em on, to rush up and get slaughtered; he put a bullet into Sam Ward's back ribs that day, for he wanted the Bar W himself, and he figgered he'd marry Elsie Ward.

"Fact, he had Torquila kidnap her and meant to pretend to save her so she'd be grateful to him. Only she was in love with a

206

bronc buster named Morton. Figger Ban Morton and his wife Elsie'll keep a sharp eye on the watershed from now on. Ward never savvied what hit him that day, thought it was a ricochet from Ross's 'jacks."

McDowell listened to the tall jigger's account of the dynamite mine, of the peonage, of Yager's attempts to cover himself.

When Jim Hatfield had finished, Cap'n McDowell put a hand on his powerful shoulder. "Callate yuh've earned a long rest," he told the Ranger. "Yuh got sorta battered up down there in Maravilla."

Then he chuckled, at the troubled darkening of Jim Hatfield's gray-green eyes. "I was goin' to pass this complaint to another Ranger," cried McDowell, "but since yuh feel that way, Jim, yuh've shore earnt the right to it. Read it." He thrust a telegram before the tall jigger.

Four men murdered here in two days. For God's sake send us the Rangers.

Later Jim Hatfield, on Goldy, headed north out of Austin. There was work to do, work for a Ranger, and Hatfield was happy as he rode to lock horns with other enemies of the Lone Star State, kept livable by the Texas Rangers.

The employees of Thorndike Press hope you have enjoyed this Large Print book. All our Thorndike, Wheeler, and Kennebec Large Print titles are designed for easy reading, and all our books are made to last. Other Thorndike Press Large Print books are available at your library, through selected bookstores, or directly from us.

For information about titles, please call:
  (800) 223-1244

or visit our Web site at:
  http://gale.cengage.com/thorndike

To share your comments, please write:
  Publisher
  Thorndike Press
  10 Water St., Suite 310
  Waterville, ME 04901

CPSIA information can be obtained
at www.ICGtesting.com
Printed in the USA
FFOW041053210113
741FF